He lifted one eyebrow. “Is that what you think this is all about? Protection? Securing a witness?”

The pulse in her wrist ticked up several notches. Could he feel it? “I’m the only witness you have right now.”

He chuckled in the back of his throat, and the low sound sent a line of tingles racing down to her toes.

“The SFPD is not in the bodyguarding business. We’re not going to put you in the Witness Protection Program. Everything I’ve done for you has been off the books and off the clock.”

She twisted her own napkin in her lap as she tilted her head back to take in his imposing figure. “Why’d you do it?”

“Do you have to ask?”

THE BRIDGE

CAROL ERICSON

For Elise and childhood
imaginations that run wild.

ISBN-13: 978-0-373-69754-0

THE BRIDGE

This edition published by arrangement with Harlequin Books S.A.

For questions and comments about the quality of this book, please contact us at CustomerService@Harlequin.com.

Printed in U.S.A.

ABOUT THE AUTHOR

Carol Ericson lives with her husband and two sons in Southern California, home of state-of-the-art cosmetic surgery, wild freeway chases, palm trees bending in the Santa Ana winds and a million amazing stories. These stories, along with hordes of virile men and feisty women, clamor for release from Carol's head. It makes for some interesting headaches until she sets them free to fulfill their destinies and her readers' fantasies. To find out more about Carol, her books and her strange headaches, please visit her website, www.carolericson.com, "where romance flirts with danger."

Books by Carol Ericson

HARLEQUIN INTRIGUE

1034—THE STRANGER AND I
1079—A DOCTOR-NURSE ENCOUNTER
1117—CIRCUMSTANTIAL MEMORIES
1184—THE SHERIFF OF SILVERHILL
1231—THE McCLINTOCK PROPOSAL
1250—A SILVERHILL CHRISTMAS
1267—NAVY SEAL SECURITY‡
1273—MOUNTAIN RANGER RECON‡
1320—TOP GUN GUARDIAN‡
1326—GREEN BERET BODYGUARD‡
1349—OBSESSION§
1355—EYEWITNESS§
1373—INTUITION§
1379—DECEPTION§
1409—RUN, HIDE**
1415—CONCEAL, PROTECT**
1450—TRAP, SECURE**
1458—CATCH, RELEASE**
1487—THE BRIDGEΩ

‡Brothers in Arms
§Guardians of Coral Cove
**Brothers in Arms: Fully Engaged
ΩBrody Law

CAST OF CHARACTERS

Sean Brody—He's a troubled homicide detective with a tragic past he's ready to shake, but a serial killer has other plans. When Sean vows to protect a beautiful witness from the killer, he risks becoming mired in his past.

Elise Duran—The would-be victim of The Alphabet Killer, she fights back, not only for her own preservation but for Sean Brody, a man in danger of succumbing to his demons.

Ray Lopez—A reporter with an unhealthy interest in the Brody tragedy, whose breakthrough story may be his last.

Courtney Chu—A therapist and Elise's best friend, she treats a lot of disturbed people in her line of work. But is one dangerously more disturbed than the others?

Dr. James Patrick—He was counselling Sean's father twenty years ago at the time of the man's suicide and may be the only person who can shed light on Joseph Brody's state of mind—if he's allowed to talk.

Detective Matt Curtis—Sean's partner basks in the limelight of Sean's feats, but maybe he wants to take center stage.

Dan Jacoby—The fingerprint tech extraordinaire is happy to leave the detective work to the detectives, but his hidden past may tell a different story.

Ty Russell—Elise's ex-fiancé may have cheated on her, but now he's had a change of heart. How much will he risk to get her back?

Marie Giardano—The SFPD records keeper has seen a lot in her thirty-five years with the department, and she has her own suspicions about the Brody tragedy, but she's afraid to share them.

Chapter One

He wanted to kill her.

"Elise."

The whispered name floated along the fog, mingled with it, surrounded her.

Her eyes ached with the effort of trying to peer through the milky white wisps that blanketed the San Francisco Bay shoreline, but if she couldn't see him, he couldn't see her.

And she planned to keep it that way.

A foghorn bellowed in the night, and she took advantage of the sound to make another move toward the waves lapping against the rocky shore. If she had to, she'd wriggle right into the frigid waters of the bay.

She flattened herself against the sand, and the grains stuck to her lip gloss. It now seemed ages ago when she'd leaned over the brightly lit vanity at the club applying it.

"Elise, come out, come out wherever you are."

His voice caused a new layer of goose bumps to form over the ones she already had from the cold, damp air. Her fingers curled around the scrubby plant to her right as if she could yank it out of the sand and use it as a weapon.

If he caught her, she wouldn't allow him to drag her back to his car. She'd fight and die here if she had to.

The water splashed and her tormenter cursed. He must've stepped into the bay. And he didn't like it.

She drove her chin into the sand to prop up her head and peered into the wall of fog. The lights on the north tower of the Golden Gate Bridge winked at her. The occasional humming of a car crossing the bridge joined with the lapping of the water as the only sounds she could hear over the drumbeat of her heart.

And his voice when he chose to speak, a harsh whisper, all traces of the refined English accent he'd affected outside the club gone.

What a fool she'd been to trust him.

Another footfall, too close for comfort. She held her breath. If he tripped over her, she'd have to run, find another place to hide in plain sight. Or at least it would be plain sight if the fog lifted.

The damp cover made her feel as if they were the only two people in this hazy world where you couldn't see your hand two inches in front of your face.

Who would break first? The fog? Her? Or the maniac trying to kill her? Because she knew he wanted to kill her. She could hear the promise in his voice.

"Elise?"

She wanted to scream at him to stop using her name in those familiar tones—as if they were old friends. Instead of predator and prey.

She didn't scream. She pressed her lips together, and the sand worked its way into her mouth. She ground it between her teeth, anger shoving the fear aside for a moment.

If this guy thought she'd give up, he'd picked the wrong target. The Durans of Montana were nobody's victims.

A breeze skittered across the bay, and debris tickled her face. White strands of fog swirled past her, and for the first time since she'd hurled herself from the trunk of her captor's car, she could see the shapes of scrubby plants emerge from the mist.

She swallowed a sob. When she'd least expected or wanted it, the cursed San Francisco fog was rolling out to sea.

A low chuckle seemed to come at her from all directions. He knew it, too.

Time to make a move.

Elise pinned her arms to her sides and propelled herself into a roll. Once she had the momentum, the rest was easy as she hit a slight decline to the water.

Arm. Back. Arm. Chest. Around and around she rolled. She squeezed her eyes shut and scooped in a breath of air. Her preparations didn't make the impact any easier.

When she hit the icy bay, she gasped, pulling in a breath and a mouthful of salty water with it. She choked it out and ducked her head beneath the small waves.

The bay accepted her in a chilly embrace, and she clawed her way along the rocky floor. Fearing the swift current, she didn't want to swim away from the shoreline, but the water might just be enough to hide her from the lunatic trying to kill her.

She popped up her head and dragged in another breath. The wind whipped around her, blowing her wet hair against her cheeks.

The fog dissipated even more, and she could make out the form of a man loping back and forth, swinging something at the ground.

She took a deep breath and went under again. The current tugged at her dress, inviting her into the bay. She resisted, scrabbling against the rocks. The current snatched her shoes anyway.

She scraped her knees on the bay floor and lifted her face to the surface, taking a sip of air. The figure on land seemed farther away. Would he be able to see her head in the water? Would he come after her?

She submerged her head again and managed a breaststroke and a scissor kick to propel herself farther from the man combing the shore.

She'd have to get out of the water soon or she'd die from hypothermia. As if to drive this truth home, her teeth began to chatter and she lost the tips of her fingers to numbness.

Once more she poked her head up from the water. The steel buttress of the bridge was visible in front of her. Maybe she could clamber on top of it to escape the cold fingers of the bay.

She twisted her head around. The man had disappeared from view. A seagull shrieked above, cutting through the rumbling of a car engine.

Elise whipped her head around. An orange service truck trundled along the road fronting the shore, its amber light on the roof revolving.

Elise screamed for the first time since her ordeal began. She clambered from the water, her dress clinging to her legs. She bunched the skirt of the dress around her waist and waded from the bay.

"Help! Stop!"

The occupants of the truck couldn't have heard her, but the truck pulled to the side of the road anyway. A door swung open.

Her frozen limbs buckled beneath her, but she willed them to support her. She rose to her feet and screamed again, waving her arms above her head. "Help! I'm in the water!"

The white oval of a face turned toward her.

Elise pumped her legs, hoping they were obeying her command to run. She tried to scream again, but her jaw locked as a shower of chills cascaded through her body.

The man in the orange jumpsuit started jogging toward her, and another orange jumpsuit joined him.

Her bare feet slogged through the sand and she kept tripping over the bushes dotting the shore, but she continued to move forward.

By the time she and the service workers met, her body was shivering convulsively.

"Oh, my God, Brock. I think we've got a jumper."

She shook her head back and forth. *Really? Would a jumper be able to swim to shore and run toward help?*

Brock joined his buddy, shrugging out of his orange jacket. "I already called 9-1-1. It's gonna be okay, lady."

He wrapped his jacket around her, and she began to sink to the ground. He caught her under the arms. "Stay with us. The ambulance should be here soon."

"How did you do it? How did you survive the jump?"

She licked the salt from her lips and worked her jaw. "I didn't jump from the bridge."

Brock tugged the coat around her tighter. "Then what the hell were you doing out there?"

As sirens wailed in the distance, she blew out a breath and closed her eyes. "Escaping a killer."

HER TOES TINGLED and she took another sip of the hot tea. When the ambulance got her to the emergency room, the nurses had stripped off her soggy dress and wrapped her in warm blankets. They'd tucked her into this bed and piled an electric blanket on top of her as well as wedged some heat packs under her arms and behind her neck.

When she could sit up, they'd brought her a cup of tea. Now Elise inhaled the lemon-scented steam from the cup and tried to relax her limbs.

Someone yanked back the curtain that separated her bed from the other beds in the emergency room. A doctor approached her with a small tablet computer clutched under his arm.

He clicked his tongue. "It's clear you're not a jumper since you don't have any injuries that would indicate you'd just hit the water at seventy-five miles per hour from a height of two hundred and twenty feet."

Elise slurped the hot tea and rolled it on her tongue before swallowing. "I told Brock and the other city worker I didn't jump. Didn't they believe me?"

"The first report was of a jumper, but the EMT said you were attacked."

She wrapped her hands around the cup as her ordeal knocked her over the head all over again. "I went into the water to avoid him."

"Boyfriend? Husband?"

Elise's jaw dropped. Everyone sure liked making assumptions. "A killer. A stranger. He abducted me from the street. I escaped."

The doctor nodded as if this was his second guess all along. "Based on the EMT's report of his conversation with you, the police are on their way."

"Here?"

"They want to question you immediately. Once you're warmed up, you're free to go." He tapped the tablet screen. "The nurse indicated you have a bump on the back of your head, too."

"He hit me, maybe with the cast he had on his arm."

"Says here you're not showing any signs of concussion and the skin on your scalp didn't break. How's the head feeling?"

"My head is the least of my worries right now."

The doctor snapped the computer shut. "You're lucky. A few more minutes in that water and you'd be dead. It was a crazy thing to do."

"A few more minutes with that maniac and I'd be dead. I figured the water gave me a better chance."

The doctor lifted his shoulders in his white coat and stepped beyond the curtain to practice his feeble bedside manner on another emergency-room patient.

Beneath her warm blankets, Elise shivered at the memory of the man stalking her. Would the police be able to find him based on her description? And how accurate was that description? The man she'd helped outside the club had spoken to her with an English accent. That accent had disappeared when he'd been searching for her on the sand. How much of his appearance was phony, too? The beard? The mustache?

"Knock, knock. Ms. Duran?"

A male voice called from outside the curtain.

"That's me."

The man brushed aside the curtain and pulled it closed behind him. "I'm Detective Brody. How are you feeling, Ms. Duran?"

"Elise. You can call me Elise. I feel…warm." And it wasn't because a fine specimen of manhood had just emerged from curtain number three. At least she didn't think it was.

"That's good after what you've been through." He pointed to the plastic chair by the wall. "May I?"

"Sure. Of course." It beat craning her neck to look up at all six feet something of him.

"They're keeping you warm enough?" He tipped his chin at the space heater glowing in the corner.

She nodded, although she wondered if she'd ever feel warm again.

Detective Brody dragged the chair to her bed and slipped out of his suit jacket. He hung it over the back of the chair, smoothing the expensive-looking material.

Hunching forward, he withdrew a notepad and pen from the pocket of his crisp white shirt.

"The EMT reported that you were out in the bay trying to escape from someone. Tell me what happened from the beginning, Elise."

His dark eyes zeroed in on her face, making her feel as if she were the only woman in the world. She shook her head. He was a policeman and she was a victim—she *was* the only woman in the world for him right now.

She took a deep breath. "I was coming out of a club on Geary Street at two in the morning—the Speakeasy. Do you know it?"

"Private club, right? Stays open past two."

"My friend got invitations from a member."

"Was your friend with you at—" he glanced at his notepad "—one-fifty?"

"I was alone. I left her inside the club."

"Had you been drinking?"

His tone got sharper and the muscles in his handsome face got tighter. She was glad she wouldn't have to disappoint him.

"One drink's my limit, and I'd had that at around eleven o'clock when we first got there."

His spiky dark lashes dropped over his eyes briefly, and Elise knew she'd just passed some test.

"How were you getting home?"

"Taxi. There's no parking in that neighborhood. I had the bartender call me a taxi, and I went outside to wait for it."

"What happened next?"

Goose bumps rippled across her arms, and she pulled the blanket up to her chin. "I saw a man standing beside a car. The trunk of the car was open."

"Did he see you? Speak to you right away?"

"I'm sure he saw me, although we didn't make eye contact. He must've seen me come out of the club, but by the time I looked at him he was bending over the open trunk."

"What kind of car? Make? Model?"

Was he serious? "I'm not sure. It was a small, dark car, old."

"Then what? Did he talk to you?"

Elise licked her lips, and she could still taste the salt from the bay. "He seemed to be struggling with something. Then he poked his head around the open trunk and asked me if I could give him a hand."

"Did you?"

"I guess I shouldn't have." She knotted her fingers, studying his face for signs he thought she was an idiot. She didn't see any.

"I walked toward him, and that's when I noticed his arm."

Detective Brody's dark brows shot up. "His arm?"

"It was in a cast."

The pen dropped from the detective's fingers and rolled under the bed. He ducked to retrieve it. When he straightened in his chair, his handsome face was flushed.

He cleared his throat. "The man's arm was in a cast?"

"A full cast almost up to his shoulder, like he had a broken arm. When he asked me for help, I…I didn't think anything of it. I wasn't suspicious, and he looked…"

"He looked what? What did he look like?"

She shrugged and the blanket slipped from one bare shoulder. "Normal. He looked normal—blond hair, kind of on the long side, jeans. Normal."

"We'll get to the rest of the description in a minute. So, what did you help him with?"

"A box." She folded her arms across her stomach, where knots were forming and tightening. "There was a box on the ground that he was trying to get into his trunk."

"And you helped him with the box?" His hand froze,

poised over his notepad, where he'd been scribbling her every word since retrieving the pen.

"I didn't get the chance." She clutched her arms, digging her nails into her skin. "When I bent over the box, he hit me on the back of the head."

Detective Brody jumped from the chair, knocking it to the floor.

"What's wrong?" His sudden movement had caused her to jerk forward, and the blanket fell from her shoulders.

"A man with a cast asked you for help and then bashed your head in. Did he stuff you in the trunk?"

"Yes, yes. Has this happened before?"

Closing his eyes, he stuffed the notepad in the pocket of his shirt. His lips barely moved as he mumbled, "A long time ago."

"What? A long time ago? Last year?" She hadn't heard about any crazed killers in the news lately. Were the cops trying to hide a serial killer from tourists?

He righted the chair, brushed off his jacket and dropped onto the hard plastic. Pinching the bridge of his nose, he said, "How'd you get out of the trunk? How'd you get away?"

Did he plan to let her know whether or not somebody was running around San Francisco abducting women?

"M-my dress must've gotten caught in the trunk when he closed it. I came to, and there was a light in the trunk."

"Wouldn't there have been some indicator on the dash that the trunk was open, alerting him?"

"I told you. It was an older car. Maybe there was no indicator. Maybe there was and he didn't notice it."

"You pushed open the trunk and jumped out?"

"Not right away. When I woke up, I was a little groggy and a lot terrified. The car was going fast, too. I waited until he slowed down. Once he did—" she pushed her hands against the air "—I shoved open the trunk and rolled out."

"Ouch."

"It beat the alternative."

"But he heard you." He dipped into his pocket and retrieved his notepad again.

"Yeah, the trunk lid sprang up, so he would've seen it. After I hit the ground and rolled, I jumped up and started running toward the shoreline, running into the fog."

"You had a couple of things going for you tonight—the dress getting caught and the heavy fog."

"I could barely see the lights on the bridge, and we were right there."

"The bridge?" A muscle ticked in the corner of his mouth.

"The Golden Gate. He was driving down that road along the strip of shoreline at the base of the bridge, or close enough to the base before you pull into the parking lot there."

"I know it." He tapped the end of the pen against his thumbnail in a nervous gesture. "You've described the car. What about the man? Did you get a good look at him?"

"He had shaggy blond hair." She skimmed her hand on the top of her shoulder. "Long. He had a full beard and mustache."

"Height and weight?"

"I have no idea. He was kind of stooped over when I joined him at the car. He could've been short, but I think he was probably medium height because he was bent over. I think he only straightened up when he was behind me."

"And was he a thin guy? Big?"

"Seemed heavyset, but he was wearing a jacket so it was hard to tell."

"Other clothing?"

"Jeans, dark shirt, that bulky gray jacket." She snapped

her fingers. "Wait. He was wearing a jacket with elastic at the sleeves and had both sleeves pushed up. That's how I saw the cast. And on the other arm, the one not in the cast, he had a tattoo."

"Perfect. What was it?"

"It was a bird, a bird with wings spread open."

The detective lifted his gaze from his notepad and drilled her with his dark eyes.

A chill zigzagged down her spine. Had she hit on something? He must know this killer. This *had* happened before.

He unbuttoned the left cuff of his pressed white shirt and pushed it up. "Do you know what kind of bird it was?"

"No—dark colors. It was hard to see. I just noticed the bird's wings."

Then he extended his forearm toward her. "Was it like this?"

A tattoo of a dark blue bird spreading his wings, his claws rising from a flame, decorated the detective's forearm.

Elise clapped a hand over her mouth and jerked back against the bed. "Exactly like that."

Chapter Two

The tattoo on Sean's arm tingled and burned. Some killer had the same tattoo? And why this killer? The M.O. of someone luring women to his car by feigning an injury and then hitting them on the head was all too familiar to him.

Familiar and painful.

Now he'd gone and scared the color out of the victim—Elise, who was shrinking against her pillow, her face as white as the sheets. He'd already startled her when he jumped from his chair, knocking it over. No need for both of them to be freaking out right now.

Sean scooped in a breath and shook down his sleeve. "Similar to that, huh?"

"Similar? Exactly the same."

Her blue eyes took up half her face, and she eyed him like a trapped animal.

He should've never shown her his tattoo. He'd completely misplaced his professional demeanor during this interview. A bird with spread wings—lots of tattoos like that out there.

"I doubt it's exactly the same, Ms. Duran."

"Elise."

"Elise." At least she still wanted him to use her first name. "You said it was dark. A bird is a bird."

She chewed her lip and then relaxed her shoulders. “Can I see it again?”

He hadn’t buttoned his cuff, so he shoved the sleeve up his arm again and rotated his forearm.

She leaned forward and her blond hair tickled the inside of his elbow. She smelled salty—not at all what he expected from this blue-eyed blonde with the peaches-and-cream skin.

She wrinkled her nose. “I guess it could’ve been different. He had a bird tattoo. You have a bird tattoo.”

He smoothed down his sleeve and buttoned the cuff. “I’m glad we got that out of the way. I wanted to show you mine to see if it would prompt any more detail.”

Actually, he hadn’t been thinking at all. What did it matter if he and a killer both had a tattoo of a bird on their arms? Unless someone was trying to pin something on him.

Just as someone pinned something on Dad.

“I…I really didn’t mean to imply that I thought it was you out there.” She twisted her damp hair into a rope over her shoulder. “The similarity just startled me. You have to admit it’s a coincidence.”

Despite the warmth of the space, he slid into his jacket. “Yeah, a coincidence. A lot of people have tattoos today, but that detail might make it easier to find this guy.”

“I hope so. I’m not his first, am I?”

“I can’t say for sure, Elise.” He tucked his notepad into his jacket pocket. “Is the hospital releasing you soon?”

“The nurse is coming back to check my temperature. If it’s at a safe level, I’m free to go.”

“It’s almost morning. How are you getting home?”

“Taxi.” She hit her forehead with the heel of her hand. “My purse. It must’ve fallen on the ground outside the club.”

“Or he took it.”

She widened her baby blues, which seemed to get even bluer. "My license is in there, my phone, my credit card."

He has her address and her contacts and God knows what else.

"If he tries to use the card, we can track him."

"He knows my address now. I got away. I can give a description of him." Her hands clawed at the sheets.

He resisted the urge to take one of those small fists in his hand. "Maybe he left the purse at the scene. We'll call the club to see if anyone found it. We're going to canvass outside the club anyway, see if he left any evidence, question the employees."

Still clutching the sheets, she said, "I'm sure he has my purse. He called my name wh-when I was hiding from him. I never told him my name."

A nurse peeked around the curtain and tiptoed to the bed in the small space. "Excuse me, Detective. I need to take her temperature."

Sean scooted his chair back to give her room, and the nurse leaned over Elise, pinching a thermometer between her fingers and wheeling the machine on the stand closer to the bed.

"I'm just going to put this under your tongue and we'll see how you're doing." The nurse made a tsking noise. "They could've done a better job drying your hair."

Elise twirled a damp lock around her finger and shrugged.

The nurse peered at the thermometer. "You're good to go. How do you feel? How's the head?"

"I'm warm, I'm dry and my head hasn't hurt since the last ibuprofen I took."

"Then I'll bring your clothes and have the doctor sign your release. I'm sorry we have to kick you out of the emergency room. You should see your own doctor as soon as possible for a once-over."

"I will, thanks."

When the nurse left, Elise clasped her hands in her lap, looking…lost.

Sean cleared his throat. "Since you don't have your purse, can I give you a lift home? Unless you want to call a friend."

Or a boyfriend? Husband? Surely this woman had someone in her life, someone to keep her safe.

"I'll take the ride, if you don't mind. My best friend is the one I went to the club with. I doubt she's going to be up at this time of the morning. I doubt she's going to be home."

"I'm assuming you lost your keys, too. How are you going to get into your place?"

"I hide a set outside."

"Not a great idea." He started to shake a finger at her, and then snatched it back. She didn't need one of his lectures on safety.

Color rushed into her pale cheeks as she dropped her gaze to her folded hands. "I guess it wasn't a great idea to approach this guy at two in the morning on a deserted street, either."

"Don't beat yourself up, Elise. He's clever. Why would you think he'd be a danger with a cast on?"

He's not the first killer to use this ploy, and he won't be the last. He had to remember that, too. The M.O. wasn't unique, just as bird tattoos weren't unique.

"I should've known. My friend, Courtney, would've known. Street smarts she'd call it."

"Is Courtney the one who stayed at the club past two and may not be home this morning?" He raised one eyebrow.

"Yeah." A smiled hovered on lips.

"Doesn't sound too street smart to me."

"Here are your clothes." The nurse had a plastic bag hanging from her wrist and a black dress dangling from her fingers. "We did our best to dry them, but I think the dress is ruined."

"Oh, well. Small price to pay." Elise took the dress from the nurse and shook it out.

Sean pushed up from the plastic chair. "I'll be in the waiting room."

It didn't take long for Elise to get dressed. After he'd circled the waiting room twice and inspected and rejected the vending machine in the corner, Elise shuffled into the waiting room, hospital slippers on her feet and a snug black dress hugging her curves.

She crossed her bare arms, and Sean strode across the room, shrugging out of his jacket. "Can't the hospital loan you a blanket for the trip home?"

"I think the nurse expected someone to pick me up and bring a change of clothes."

He draped his jacket around her shoulders. "Do you want me to call someone for you?"

"It's too early in the morning to call anyone."

"Family?"

"None here."

"Boyfriend?"

"Nonexistent."

At least he'd gotten that out of the way. He pulled the jacket tight under her chin. It was as if her assailant had known she was alone. Maybe this wasn't a random attack.

He pointed to her feet. "Can you walk in those things?"

"If I don't pick up my feet, they're surprisingly comfortable. My shoes have been swept out to sea by now."

Sean had parked his unmarked car in the small driveway in front of the emergency room entrance. He guided Elise to the car with a hand on the small of her back. Comfortable or not, it looked as if she could trip over those slippers at any minute.

He opened the front passenger door for her and she

ducked in the car, tugging at her short dress. Had it shrunk after her dip in the bay? The black, sparkly material barely covered her assets—not that he minded.

He cranked on the heater after cranking on the engine. "Are you warm enough?"

"I'm fine." She wiggled her toes and tapped on the window. "Maybe we'll get some clear weather today."

"That fog saved you last night, or rather earlier this morning."

"It did." She pinned her hands, completely covered by the sleeves of his jacket, between her bouncing knees.

"Where to?" He rolled away from the curb, looking over his left shoulder.

"Sunset District. I live in a house—the owner has the upstairs and I get the downstairs. It was divided into two apartments."

"Okay, just give me directions as we get closer." He scratched his chin. He didn't want to keep bringing up the attack, but that's why he was here, wasn't it?

"We need you at the station sometime today to work with a sketch artist. Even if the guy was wearing a disguise, maybe we can get down the shape of his face or some other distinguishing characteristic."

"Like the tattoo."

The pulse in his throat jumped. "Yeah, like the tattoo."

"Do you mind if we stop on the way for a coffee or something hot? Just a takeout."

"Sorry." He drummed the steering wheel with his thumbs. "I should've thought of that. You probably still need something warm to drink."

As he swung into a U-turn, Elise said, "Hot chocolate."

"Hot chocolate it is."

"With whipped cream."

"Of course."

She bit her lip. "I suppose I should learn to like coffee like a grown-up, but there's something so comforting about hot chocolate."

"After the experience you had, you deserve comfort." And protection. And whipped cream.

"I don't have to go in like this, do I?" She yanked at the hem of her dress, which had hitched up around her thighs.

"I'm parking right out front. You can wait in the car."

"One of the perks of riding with a cop."

He parked the car illegally at the curb and hopped out. Even though the sun was rising on the busy street and people bustled in and out of the busy coffeehouse, Sean kept his focus on his car and Elise's profile through the window.

She must've been terrified coming to in that trunk. Despite her soft, feminine appearance, she had to be made of steel to have waded into the San Francisco Bay to avoid her captor.

Holding a cup of hot chocolate in one hand and a coffee in the other, he nudged open the door and strode toward the car. Before he reached the door, Elise hopped out and took both cups from him.

"Which is which?"

"Yours is on the right."

She bent over into the car to secure his coffee in the cup holder. As she did so, her skimpy dress slid up dangerously high.

She backed out of the car, one hand flattening the dress against her thighs. When she straightened up, she rolled her eyes. "This dress was a lot longer when I started out last night."

"I believe you." He rubbed her arms as if to erase her goose bumps. "You shouldn't be out here without my jacket, anyway."

"I couldn't figure out how to roll down the window. Must be locked." She licked her lips and gave a little shiver—more like a wiggle.

It was the sexiest combination of moves ever aimed at him, and she didn't even mean it—didn't mean it as a come-on anyway.

"Get back in the car and wrap your hands around that hot chocolate. I asked for extra whipped cream."

She scurried around to the other side of the car and huddled in his jacket again, one hand darting out to grab her cup.

She slurped a sip through the lid and closed her eyes. "Perfect."

"Are you up for a few more questions?"

Her slim fingers tightened around the cup, but she nodded. "Absolutely."

"Have you been having trouble with anyone? Gotten into any arguments? Coworkers? Neighbors?"

She snorted. "You think someone put out a hit on me?"

"Just covering all bases, Elise. What kind of work do you do?"

"I'm a teacher, a kindergarten teacher."

Her students must love her sweet sincerity. You couldn't fool kids that age.

"No trouble at the school?"

"Everyone's great, no politics on the playground."

"What about your landlord?"

"Oscar? He travels a lot. We get along great. I pay my rent on time and don't have any wild parties. He's my friend's brother. That's how I met her, Courtney."

"Ex-boyfriends? Ex-husbands?"

She sipped her cocoa—too long.

"No." She sucked in a breath. "It's beautiful."

"What?" He jerked his head to the side.

"The bridge. I've been here for almost a year now, and it always takes my breath away when I get an unexpected view of it."

Sean grunted.

"They thought I was a jumper, you know."

He gripped the steering wheel. "Who?"

"The city workers who discovered me. They thought I'd jumped from the bridge. How crazy is that?"

Sean's eye twitched and he dug his knuckles into his eye to stop it. "Crazy. Chances are you wouldn't be walking out of the water if you had."

"I know there have been a few survivors, but I don't think they swam to shore on their own." She snuggled deeper into his jacket. "What would make someone do that?"

Sean lifted his tight shoulders. "Only they know. Right or left?"

She blinked her eyes. "Keep going straight, and then make a right at the next signal."

"So, no bad blood between you and anyone?"

"No. I…I don't like to fight—typically."

Except for her life.

She guided him the rest of the way to her house, and he parked on the street. Single-family homes lined the block, but he could tell several of them were conversions.

She shrugged off his jacket and shoved her feet into the paper slippers. "Thank you, Detective Brody. Will you call me to let me know what time to come down to the station? If you give me something to write on, I'll jot down my home phone number. I guess my cell is gone."

Did she really think he'd drop her curbside while some lunatic had her purse, her address and her keys?

"I'll walk you up."

She thrust her arms into the sleeves of his jacket and scrambled from the car, holding on to her cup.

She led him to the side of the house and through a gate onto a brick walkway. Holding up her finger, she dipped beside a planter. She raked through the dirt and pulled out a key.

He'd seen better hiding places, but at least she hadn't stashed the key beneath the welcome mat.

She puckered her lips and blew on the key before inserting it into the dead bolt. It clicked.

The key scraped when she pulled it out of the lock, and Sean's stomach knotted with the sound. He cinched her wrist as she reached for the doorknob.

"Wait. Me first."

Her gaze darted to the door and back to his face. She dipped her chin and stumbled back.

He withdrew his weapon from his shoulder holster and edged open the door. Coiling his muscles, he stepped into Elise's house.

The rising sun filtered through the slats of her blinds, throwing a vertical pattern across the deep blue carpet on the floor. A low light glowed beneath a whimsical lampshade painted with flowering vines. Colorful children's books littered a coffee table in the shape of a piece of driftwood.

Sean eased out a slow breath and took another step into the inviting room. "Everything look okay in here?"

She peered around his body, nudging his arm with her head. "Looks fine to me."

Something scratched at the sliding glass door, and Elise grabbed his biceps, digging her nails into the material of his shirt. She released a noisy sigh along with his arm and pointed to the door. "My mangy friend is looking for a handout."

A gray-and-white-striped cat pawed at the door again, flicked his tail and walked away.

"How many rooms?"

"This one." She waved an arm in front of her. "You can see the kitchen, and then there are two bedrooms and a bathroom down the hall. That door leads to the garage."

"That would be a good place to start." Sean swung

open the door to the garage. A little hybrid crouched in the center of the garage floor and well-ordered shelves surrounded it. A washer and dryer were tucked in a corner. Not many places to hide here. He took a look under the car for the heck of it.

"Let's have a look in the bedrooms just to be on the safe side."

"I'm all for safe."

She led the way down the short hallway, and Sean tried really hard to drag his gaze away from her swaying hips and the dress that seemed to be shrinking by the minute.

The doors to both bedrooms yawned open, and after a cursory look at the rooms and in the closets, Elise assured him all was well.

She traipsed down the hall to the bathroom at the end, calling over her shoulder. "It's a good thing I have a small house."

She tripped to a stop at the bathroom door and gasped. "Oh!"

With his heart thudding, Sean took two giant steps to join her. The room tilted and he slammed a hand against the doorjamb to stop the spinning.

Elise hooked a finger through his belt loop. "Wh-what does it mean?"

Sean's eyes burned as he read the words on the bathroom mirror in red lipstick: *Here we go again, Brody.*

"I don't know what it means."

Sean ran the back of his hand across his mouth.

Oh, but he did. He knew exactly what it meant.

Chapter Three

Elise's gaze edged from the lipstick words on her mirror to the cop's reflection. *Brody*—that was his name. Why had someone scrawled it on her bathroom mirror along with a cryptic message?

She loosened her hold on his belt loop and crept closer to the vanity. Wedging her hands on the tile, she leaned toward the words on the glass.

"Don't touch anything."

"Oops!" She snatched her hands off the vanity. "Do you think he left fingerprints?"

"Maybe."

The color had returned to Detective Brody's face, but his expression remained hard and tight, alert. The tension vibrating from his body wrapped her in its coils, creating an ache in her shoulders.

She coughed. "It's him, isn't it? The man who abducted me."

"He has, or at least had, your purse and your driver's license. He found your house and used your key to get inside."

His matter-of-fact words socked her in the gut. She sank to the edge of the tub and folded over to pin her forehead onto her knees.

Detective Brody crouched beside her, curling one warm

hand around her bare calf. "You need to get your locks changed and get out of here for now."

Poor small-town girl lost in the big city. Everyone back home had predicted she wouldn't last six months here. She'd doubled that and would continue to prove them wrong.

Hot anger cascaded through her body, and she curled her hands into fists. She jerked her head up and pushed the hair out of her face. Time to take control of this situation.

She hadn't been Ty's victim back in Montana, and she didn't plan to be anyone's victim here in San Francisco despite what her family feared. It started with answers. It started with Brody.

She planted a finger on Detective Brody's granitelike chest. "Why is this guy communicating with you? How does he even know you're on this case?"

He blinked, his spiky lashes and dark eyes momentarily distracting her from her purpose.

Her finger drilled farther into his starched shirt. "I want some straight answers. Is this guy a serial killer? Has he been communicating with you?"

Brody shifted away from the accusatory finger and rose to his feet, smoothing imaginary wrinkles from his gray slacks. "The only serial killer we have at work right now in the city is a guy killing transients. You're hardly his typical victim."

She ground her teeth together. "I'm nobody's victim. I got away, remember?"

"I do." He raised his eyebrows.

She didn't expect him to understand the vehemence behind her words, and she didn't care what he thought about it. "So, why is this guy sending you messages via my bathroom mirror? How did he know you'd be here, in my house?"

"A lot of serial killers follow other cases." He shoved his

hands in his pockets and lifted his shoulders. "I've been a homicide detective in the city for several years. My name's been in the papers a few times. He obviously knows who I am and correctly figured I'd be working this case."

Her gaze slid to his forearm, where the sleeve of his shirt hid the bird tattoo. Then she looked into his dark eyes, shuttered and secretive. Weren't the criminals supposed to be the ones with the secrets, not the cops?

"And he knew you'd be here?"

"Maybe not, but he assumed you'd tell the cops about his little message." He pulled a cell phone from his pocket. "I'm going to call this in, get a tech down here to dust for fingerprints."

His expression and tone told her she'd get nothing more out of him. She smacked her hand against the doorjamb. "And I'm going to get my locks changed."

"You're going to stay here, in this house?"

She wedged her hands on her hips. "Where would I go? I'm a kindergarten teacher, not an heiress like London Breck. I can't afford to camp out in a hotel until you catch this guy… *If* you catch this guy."

"How about staying with a friend?"

"Indefinitely?" She jerked her thumb at the ceiling. "I have Oscar."

"Oscar?"

"Oscar Chu, my landlord." She formed a gun with her fingers and pointed at him. "I also have my .22."

"You have a gun?"

"It's in my closet and it's unloaded, but yeah I have a gun and I know how to use it." A smile pulled at one side of his mouth, and Elise narrowed her eyes. "You find it funny that I have a handgun? I can assure you it's all legal."

"I find it…awesome." He tilted his phone toward her. "Get someone out here to change your locks then, and I'll get a tech to dust for fingerprints in case this guy got even more careless than writing a message on a mirror."

She tiptoed down the hallway and ducked into her office to retrieve her laptop to look up locksmiths in the area.

"After you call the locksmith, why don't you check around to see if anything is missing? I'll take a look at your doors and windows."

She tapped her computer and called out, "My laptop's still here, and I don't think you're going to find any signs of a break-in. It's pretty apparent he used my key to get in."

"Look around anyway."

She pulled open a drawer in her dining nook where she kept a camera and her MP3 player. Both were undisturbed. "I don't think he was interested in stealing anything, just game playing."

"Obviously, he used your key. I'm not checking your doors and windows to see how he got in."

She returned to the bathroom door with the laptop tucked under one arm. "What for then?"

Brody balanced on the edge of her tub and peered at the small frosted window above it. "I'm just making sure he didn't rig something so he can get back in once you change the locks."

She shivered and hugged the computer to her chest. "I'm glad someone's mind works that way."

"Keep looking. Maybe he left something behind." He jumped from the tub, surprisingly light on his feet for a big guy.

She settled the laptop on the kitchen table and did a search for locksmiths. She placed a call to one who worked weekends and made emergency calls.

While Brody continued checking the doors and windows, Elise rifled through her drawers and closets. She didn't find anything amiss, but the thought of that maniac in her house gave her pause every once in a while, and she had to close her eyes to catch her breath.

She had no intention of telling her folks back home about this. She could picture the pinched faces and I-told-you-so's already. They didn't need to know. Of course, there'd be no hiding it if she wound up dead.

A figure moved across her window, and she gasped and crossed her hands over her heart. She crept closer and let out a long breath when she saw Brody poking around the plants by the sliding glass door.

She rapped on the glass, and he looked up. He'd tossed his tie over his shoulder and rolled up his shirt sleeves, his tattoo peeking from the cuff.

She wouldn't mind seeing that sight out her window every morning.

She unlocked the window and shoved up the sash. Pressing her nose to the mesh screen, she called out, "Find anything weird?"

He thrust one arm into the tangle of flowers and withdrew a blue ball of glass. He cradled it in his hands, lifting it as if in offering. "Just this. What is it?"

Her face warmed, but he probably couldn't see her heightened color through the screen. "It's just some decoration."

The woman at the psychic shop in The Haight had told her it would ward off evil. Guess the killer with the fake English accent hadn't come through the backyard.

Someone knocked on the front door.

"That's either your guy or my locksmith."

"Don't answer it yet. Wait for me."

She slammed the window shut and rubbed her fingers together to brush away the dust.

Detective Brody stepped through the sliding glass door from the patio and strode to the front of the house. Leaning forward, he placed his eye at the peephole. "That's my guy."

He swung open the door. "You're fast, Jacoby."

"So are you." The short, powerfully built man hoisted a black bag off his shoulder. "You haven't even written your report yet and you're working the case."

Detective Brody pointed down her hallway. "The man who abducted Ms. Duran made his way back to her place and left a message on the mirror." He gestured to Elise. "This is Elise Duran, the vic—the woman who got away."

His words caused a warm glow in her tummy. A man who listened.

"I'm Dan Jacoby, fingerprint tech extraordinaire." They shook hands and he squeezed her fingertips as if trying to get a read on her pads. "You're one brave lady."

"Nice to meet you, and I did what anyone would do to get away." She waved a hand behind her. "Do you want to see the mirror first?"

"After you."

Jacoby followed her so closely, she tugged on the hem of her skirt. She really needed to put on some clothes.

Elise led the two men to her bathroom and pushed the door wide, not that the small space could accommodate all three of them. Side by side, the shoulders of the two men could practically span the room.

Jacoby whistled through his teeth. "You failed to mention he'd left the message for you, Brody."

"Yeah, one of these megalomaniacs seeking attention. He's not happy just committing murder. He wants to make sure everyone knows how smart he is."

"The joys of being a homicide detective. These nut jobs know your names, follow your careers." Jacoby dropped his bag on the tile floor. "Give me my fingerprints and anonymity."

While Jacoby unzipped the bag, Brody tugged on her

arm. "Let's give him some room to work, unless you want to watch."

She backed out of the bathroom. "That's okay. I'll wait for my locksmith."

She didn't know if it was Jacoby's muscles or personality, but his presence overpowered the bathroom.

A few minutes later, there was a knock on the door.

Again, Brody went to it first and peered through the peephole. He opened the door a crack. "Yeah?"

"Someone called for a locksmith." The locksmith held out a card between two fingers.

Brody plucked it from his grip and showed it to Elise.

She nodded. "That's the company I called."

Brody widened the door, and the locksmith stamped his feet on the mat outside.

"Show me what you need."

"All locks with a key, changed." Elise twisted the doorknob. "Starting with this one, as well as the dead bolt. There's an interior door to the garage, too. Same key."

"Can you show me some ID?" He eyed Detective Brody. "You're not the only careful ones around here. We have to look up the title to the house and verify the owner."

Elise twisted her fingers. "I'm not the owner. The owner lives upstairs and he's not home."

The locksmith squinted at a piece of paper in his hands. "Who's the owner?"

"Oscar Chu."

"Yep. That's what I have here."

"I can give you his cell. He'll vouch for me."

Detective Brody stepped between her and the locksmith, whipping out his badge. "I'll vouch for her. I'm Detective Sean Brody, and Ms. Duran needs her locks changed for security reasons."

The locksmith scratched his jaw as he eyed the badge. "If you say so."

Elise pressed her lips together as she led the locksmith to the door leading to the garage. While she felt grateful that Detective Brody had intervened and smoothed the way for her to get her locks changed, his take-charge attitude on her behalf left a sour taste in her mouth. She'd had her fill of it from her father and brothers.

Shaking her head, she rolled back her shoulders. This situation bore little resemblance to the way the male members of her family had tried to control her life. This was a matter of life and death, not marriage and betrayal.

And here she thought she'd gotten over the "all men are scum" stage.

She tapped the garage door. "Just match the dead bolts and door handle locks for the garage and the front door, and give me two keys—three. I'd better give one to Oscar."

"You got it." The locksmith dropped to his knees, his toolbox clinking and clanking as he set it on the floor next to him.

Elise wandered back to the bathroom, where Detective Brody was parked against the door jamb. "Anything interesting?"

Jacoby looked up, running a hand over his shaved head. "Nope. Looks like one set of prints, and I'm assuming they're yours. Do you live alone?"

"Yes." And that was all she had to say on the subject. She slid a glance at Brody, who was intently watching the tech's work. She hadn't brought a date back to her house since moving to San Francisco.

She didn't trust these smooth-talking city boys much. If she couldn't read a boy she'd known all her life back home in Montana, what chance did she have figuring out some metrosexual urban dweller?

Since Brody seemed consumed with interest in what Jacoby was doing, Elise took the opportunity to assess the detective—not the metrosexual type at all, although he had the clothes. After a year of hanging out with Courtney, she'd learned to recognize an expensive suit when she saw one. The drape of Brody's suit screamed custom-tailored, but the fine material and precise cut couldn't mask the naked power of the man.

He practically hummed with purpose and strength—a man's man her brothers would call him. If her brothers approved of him, that might be reason enough to steer clear, but Brody didn't possess any of the cockiness and good old boyness that characterized her brothers and Ty.

Steer clear? She'd let her imagination get way ahead of her. She didn't have to steer clear of or move in on Detective Brody. He was a cop investigating a crime—a crime aimed at her. Heck, he could be married for all she knew. A surreptitious inventory of his left hand suggested otherwise.

Jacoby tossed the last of his implements in his bag, and Elise jumped.

Detective Brody made a half turn and cupped her elbow. "Still nervous? Even when the locksmith changes the locks, you don't have to stay here. You don't have anything to prove—to me."

Elise swallowed. Had she been so transparent? "Is the SFPD going to foot the bill for my room at the Fairmont?"

"Uh, no."

"Then it looks like I'm digging in here."

"Before I take a look at the doors and windows, press your index finger on the pad and then roll it onto this card." Jacoby held out a small white ink pad cupped in his palm and a card pinched between the fingers of his other hand. "Just want to have your fingerprints on file to compare with these."

She plucked the pad from his hand and pressed her finger against the smooth ink. "I'm a teacher. My fingerprints are already on file."

"That helps. And teachers are the best. My mom was a teacher." Smiling, he put the card on the vanity, and she rolled her finger from right to left.

Jacoby tucked the pad and card in a side pocket of his bag and then patted it. "All set. I'm just going to take a quick look at the front door."

They watched his work for several more minutes and then Detective Brody hovered over the locksmith, asking a million questions.

Elise smirked. The guy probably couldn't wait to finish up this job.

Jacoby came in from the patio and hoisted his bag over his broad shoulder. "Nothing much of anything."

"Thanks, Dan. Send me your findings, and I'll include them in my report."

When he reached the door, Jacoby turned. "I'm glad you're okay. This could be the work of a serial killer. Your attack could be linked to that woman's body we found dumped near the Presidio."

Elise whipped her head around toward Detective Brody. "I thought you said there'd been nothing matching this M.O.?"

He shot a dark look at Jacoby, who shrugged. "We know very little about that murder. It could be related to the transient killings."

"That woman had a bump on the back of her head, too. He could've hit her and stuffed her in a trunk before he did…other things."

A frisson of fear tickled her spine, but Elise preferred to concentrate on the anger boiling her blood. "It sure sounds like it could be related. Why is the SFPD hiding these murders? Women have a right to know if they're being hunted down in the streets."

"Stop." Detective Brody crossed his two index fingers, one over the other. "You've both made a lot of leaps here.

We're not hiding anything. That murder had a couple of columns in the paper. Maybe you skipped the front page that day."

Elise sucked in her bottom lip. She didn't even get the newspaper. She got most of her news from the internet, and she had to admit she didn't search for murder stories.

"Miss?" The locksmith poked his head around the corner of the hallway. "The garage door's done. I'm going to start on the front door."

"Perfect." Elise opened the door for Jacoby. "I suppose you're not going to find anything from the evidence you collected. He wouldn't go to all the trouble of letting himself into my house to scrawl messages and then leave a nice set of his fingerprints."

"You're probably right, but I'll let Sean here know if I find anything out of the ordinary. He's the man."

He swung his bag from one shoulder to the other and saluted as he walked to the sidewalk.

Elise stepped away from the door, leaving it open for the locksmith. "What now?"

"I'll wait for him to finish with your locks, and then I have to go back to the station to write up my report."

"Do you want to tell me about that other woman? The one dumped by the Presidio?"

"Not really. You don't want to hear the gory details."

"How do you know?" Tugging at the hem of her dress, she sat on the arm of the couch. "I'm tougher than I look, you know."

"I have no doubt about that. Anyone who can escape a killer by wading into the San Francisco Bay is hard as nails."

"I would've done anything to escape him." She folded her arms across her chest. "So why do you think I can't handle the details of a murder?"

He rubbed his eye with his knuckle. "Because it's ugly

and sordid. Why invite that into your world when it doesn't have to be there? There are some images that you can never erase from you mind."

She gripped her upper arms, digging her nails into her flesh. He should know. Maybe she *didn't* want to hear the particulars.

Voices at the door had Elise raising her eyebrows at Brody. He headed across the room first, blocking her view.

The locksmith rose. "This guy's looking for Ms. Duran. Says he found her stuff."

Elise's steps quickened. "Really? My purse?"

A man dressed in running shorts and a sweaty T-shirt held up her small black bag from last night. "I found this on the street, a few blocks up. I looked inside, found your license and knew the address was back this way."

She moved forward, hands extended. "Thank you."

"Wait." Brody handed her a white handkerchief. "In case he left prints."

As she poked around in the purse, Brody asked, "What time did you find it?"

"Just now. Maybe five minutes ago." The runner was already backing down the porch.

"Can I get your name and address?"

"Hey, man, I didn't steal the purse."

Brody held up a hand with his badge cupped in the palm. "I'm not accusing you of anything, just in case we have further questions."

Hopping from one foot to the other, the man gave Brody his name and address and then took off at a sprint.

The locksmith pointed his drill at the runner's retreating form. "Nervous, huh?"

Brody took her arm and steered her back to the kitchen. "Anything missing?"

"Let's see." She held up her hand and counted off from the first finger. "My money, my keys, my lipstick."

"Your lipstick?" He jerked his thumb over his shoulder toward the bathroom.

"Different shade, but now that makes two of my lipsticks he's stolen."

"Even if he hadn't kept your keys, you would've still had to change your locks since he got a look at your license."

"I know." She slipped her cell phone from the bag. "At least he left me my phone."

She glanced at the display and noticed two text messages blinking. "Do you want something to eat or drink while we're waiting for the locks?"

"Just some water, please."

She placed the phone and handkerchief on the kitchen counter and went to the refrigerator to fill a glass with water from the dispenser. She clinked the glass in front of him and swept her phone from the tile.

She opened the first message, which Courtney had sent earlier this morning. One word—*breakfast?* If Courtney thought she had a lot to tell Elise about last night, Elise definitely had her beat.

She clicked on the next message from an unknown number. Someone had sent her a picture. A wisp of apprehension brushed the back of her neck as she touched the picture to expand it.

The eyes of the girl in the picture mesmerized her, and she felt darkness closing in around her.

Chapter Four

Elise dropped the phone. The corner hit the counter and bounced once before landing facedown. Her body convulsed, and then she began to sway.

"Elise?" He caught her with one arm, supporting her against his chest. He barely felt the pressure from her tiny frame. Was she having some kind of delayed shock or reaction to the hypothermia?

He started to lead her out of the kitchen, but she dug her heels in the floor.

"The phone." The rasp in her voice made it sound as if she were choking.

"Sit first. I'll get the phone in a second." He swept her up in his arms and carried her to the couch. Her dress had hiked up nearly around her waist, exposing an expanse of smooth thigh and a pair of wrinkled black panties.

He settled her on the couch and dragged a colorful afghan across her lap. "What's on the phone?"

He charged back into the kitchen. Had her abductor sent her a message, too? Good. The better to track him down.

Her teeth chattered. "I-it's a p-picture."

Sean snapped on a rubber glove and touched the screen, bringing it to life. He swore at the image—a young woman, bound, her eyes wide and terrified above her gag.

"Do you know her?"

"Wh-what?"

Sean sat beside Elise and wrapped an arm around her shoulder, pressing her close against his body. Gradually, her trembling subsided.

He rubbed her arm. "Do you know the woman in the picture?"

She shook her head, and her hair, still stiff from the salt water, scratched his cheek.

"The number. Do you recognize the telephone number?"

"No." She took a deep breath that caused a shudder to run through her body. "It came up as unknown. He sent that to me, that vile, horrible…" Her words broke off in a sob.

"Shh." He wrapped his other arm around her so that he enfolded her in a hug, and still the ripples coursed through her.

She tilted her head back and stared into his face. "She's in the trunk of a car, isn't she? Just like me."

"It looks like it. He's an idiot. He's allowed his hubris to get the better of him. We're going to blow up this picture, trace the phone number. He's just given us a bunch of evidence we didn't have before."

"And the girl? Do you think she's dead?"

Of course she was dead. "I don't know, Elise. It doesn't look good."

"That could've been me. That *was* me, only he didn't tie me up. Maybe he perfected his technique after I got away."

"We have no idea when this picture was taken. I don't think he went out after you escaped this morning and found another woman."

This morning. Did all this just happen today? She chewed on her bottom lip. "I want it off my phone."

"I know you do." He stuffed the phone in his pocket.

"But right now the picture is evidence, and so is your phone. We need to find that girl."

"Have there been any missing girls reported?"

"Always." He didn't plan to tell Elise about all the sad stories that crossed their desks, all the calls from desperate family members. He traced the edges of her phone with the pads of his fingers. Which family members would claim this one?

"Why did he send that to me?" Elise buried her face in her hands. "I'll never be able to get that image out of my head."

"He's a sadist." And somehow he'd dialed into him. Maybe the killer knew about his past, maybe he didn't, but now they were tied together. That message on the mirror tied them together.

"Ms. Duran, I'm all done with the locks on the front door." The locksmith poked his head around the front door. If he'd heard any of their conversation, he gave no sign.

Elise tried the locks and then settled the bill with him, but it was obvious her mind remained on that picture on her phone.

"He's a serial killer, isn't he? He's a serial killer you don't know about yet. He's just getting started and he wants to play some sick game with you…and now me."

It was a game he knew too well. He gestured around the small house. "Are you going to be okay here? I have to get to the station, turn in your phone and purse."

She glanced over her shoulder toward the hallway. "I have to take a shower."

"Do you want me to wait here? When you're done, I can take you to the station with me and you can look through some mug shots."

"Would you do that?" She was already moving toward the back rooms. "I won't be long."

He waved a hand. "Take your time. I'm going to call in

and report this picture. Maybe they can get a trace started when I give them your phone number."

She ducked into her bedroom and then darted across the hall to the bathroom, clutching a bundle of clothes to her chest.

Sean let out a long breath and collapsed onto Elise's colorful couch. What the hell was going on? Why did the guy who abducted Elise share a similar tattoo with him? Why did he write a message to him on Elise's mirror? This had to be a coincidence.

Serial killers had toyed with homicide detectives way before his father's time, and they'd continue to do so long after Sean's career. When he saw the message, Dan Jacoby hadn't jumped to any conclusions and Dan definitely knew the story of his past.

He was probably overreacting. That's what his brothers would tell him, but as the eldest the burden had weighed most heavily on him. Hell, Judd could barely even remember the old man, couldn't remember the life they'd had before...before everything had been sucked into the bay by a strong, merciless current.

He plowed his fingers through his hair and shifted to the end of the couch. The soft cushions made it tough to sit up straight, so he gave up and slouched against the back of the couch while he made his call.

When he heard the water in the shower shut off, he struggled off the couch and began to pace the small room.

Elise emerged from the bathroom on a cloud of fragrant steam. She'd pulled her blond hair into a ponytail and had replaced her ridiculously small dress with a pair of tight jeans and a beige cable sweater, giving her a blond-on-blond look that made her jaw-droppingly beautiful. He kept his jaw in place.

"Do you still think it's a good idea to stay here on your own?"

"Probably not. I'm going to have to change my cell phone number when I get that new phone." She slid a knotted scarf from the back of a chair. "I don't want any more surprises from this guy."

She headed to the door leading to the garage, and Sean stopped. "You're not coming with me?"

"I think it's easier for me to take my car, so I don't have to bother you for a ride back here."

"It's no bother." Bother? He didn't want to let Elise out of his sight.

She slid her new key in and out of the dead bolt. "I decided I'm going to call my friend Courtney to see if I can crash at her place for a few days. If it's okay with her, I'm going to head over there this afternoon."

"Good idea. Follow me to the station, and you can park in the lot there."

He sat in his idling car until Elise's garage door opened and her little hybrid rolled down the driveway. He kept an eye on his rearview mirror, stopping at every yellow light.

He sure as hell hoped the killer's fascination with Elise came to an end soon. He could bring it to an end sooner rather than later if he caught this guy. Then he could find out why he was sending him personal messages.

He cruised into the station's parking garage with Elise close on his tail. The morning shift had already gone out, depleting the ranks of patrol cars waiting in their slots.

Sean swung into an empty space at the end of the row, and Elise parked next to him.

"We're really in the bowels of the police station here, aren't we?"

"Shh, don't tell anyone we have all this parking down here." He led her to the elevator, and after a short ride, the doors opened onto a corridor bustling with both cops in and out of uniform and civilians.

He nodded at a few people on his way to homicide, trying not to read suspicion in their eyes. He'd have to lose this paranoia if he hoped to catch this guy and help Elise. Because he did want to help Elise.

He pulled out a chair on the other side of his cluttered desk. "Have a seat. I'm taking your phone to the lab, and I'll try to round up a sketch artist. We might have to call one in. Coffee? Water?"

"I'm fine." She folded her hands in her lap, her wide eyes taking in the activity of the room.

Yanking a binder from his drawer, he said, "You can pass the time looking at mug shots."

He left Elise running her finger across the plastic inserts in the binder. He dropped off the phone with instructions to print, blow up and distribute the picture the killer had sent. He put the word out for a sketch artist, and then he stopped by the coffee machine.

By the time he returned to his desk, Elise was halfway through the six-packs of mug shots in the binder he'd left with her.

Flipping a page, she looked up at his approach.

"Any luck?" He dropped into his chair and loosened his tie.

"No." She tapped the book. "Who are these guys, again?"

"Killers, rapists, batterers."

She flinched and jerked her hand back from the page. "Why are they out on the streets?"

"They did the crime and then did their time." His hand tightened around his coffee cup. "I rounded up a sketch artist for you. Do you want to give it a try after you finish looking at those mug shots?"

"Sure, although I don't know how much help I'm going to be. It was dark, and he wore a disguise—I'm positive about that. I should've realized that much facial hair was concealing something."

Elise seemed determined to blame herself and her naïveté for the attack. He couldn't sit back and allow her to browbeat herself.

He pushed away his coffee, and it sloshed over the edge. "The majority of men who have beards and moustaches are not criminals or trying to hide anything. That's not a clue that anyone would've picked up on."

Her face awash in pink, Elise smacked the book of six-packs closed. "None of these guys looks even vaguely familiar to me except one who's the spitting image of my geometry teacher, and I'm probably just projecting because I hated geometry."

A smile tugged at the corner of his mouth. "I doubt your geometry teacher is moonlighting as a criminal in San Francisco from…wherever it is you're from."

"Montana. Is it so obvious I'm not from the city?"

It was to him. She lacked that brittle edge so many urbanites had. But far be it from him to stoke the image she had of herself as the country bumpkin in the big, bad city.

He shrugged. "Not at all. I think you mentioned living here for just a year."

Nodding, she relaxed her shoulders and slumped against the back of the chair.

Sean picked up the receiver of his phone and punched the button for one of the interrogation rooms. Tony Davros, the sketch artist, picked up. "You're already there. You must be ready for the witness."

Sean pushed back his chair as he stood up, dropping the receiver back in the cradle. "Let's see what you can give us on this guy."

Elise followed him to the interrogation room, her head cranking from side to side as they waded through ringing phones, shouts across the room and people crisscrossing the space with papers or files clutched in their hands.

She wrinkled her nose. "It's noisier than a kindergarten classroom in here."

"Probably about the same level of maturity, too." He pushed open the door to the interrogation room and ushered her inside.

Davros stood up and extended his hand. "I'm Tony Davros, Ms. Duran. Wish we were meeting under happier circumstances."

Sean raised one eyebrow in Davros's direction. That's the most words he'd heard from the artist's mouth in almost two years. Davros had even pulled out a chair for Elise.

First Jacoby and now the sketch artist. He got it. Elise's fresh-faced, angelic appearance spurred men on to chivalrous deeds, prompting them to pull out chairs and hand over jackets. Even the typically surly Davros wasn't immune.

"Me, too." She shook Davros's hand and dropped onto the wooden chair. "I'm afraid the man was wearing a disguise—beard, wig, glasses, even a phony accent."

"That's not uncommon." Davros swept his palm across a piece of sketch paper and caressed his pencil. "We'll start with the shape of his face—what you could see of it."

The two of them went back and forth for several minutes, the artist coaxing and praising as his pencil moved swiftly across the page in front of him.

Shoving his hands in his pockets, Sean sauntered to where Davros sat hunched over his sketch pad, the tip of his tongue lodged in the corner of his mouth as he further defined the nose of the suspect.

Sean squinted at the face. Would someone be able to recognize him without the beard and moustache? Davros's job entailed drawing another picture without the facial hair and glasses, perhaps with shorter hair.

"That's close to what I remember." Elise tossed her ponytail over her shoulder as she leaned over the drawing.

A sharp rap at the door interrupted them, and before

Sean could even offer an invitation, it swung open and banged against the wall.

Sergeant Curtis from homicide, his eyes bugging out, thrust his head into the room. “We just got a call from patrol about a dead body, and I think you’re going to want to head out there, Brody.”

Sean’s heart slammed against his rib cage. “And why is that?”

“It’s the girl in the picture.”

Chapter Five

The blood rushed to Elise's head and she gripped the edge of the table as the room spun. She had a picture of a dead woman on her phone.

He'd killed her. He abducted her, took her picture and murdered her. And he sent that picture to her.

"How do you know it's the same person?" Detective Brody had straightened up to his full height and his body seemed coiled for action. The waves of his tension reverberated off the walls of the small room.

The cop who'd delivered the news gripped the doorknob. "As soon as you forwarded the picture to us, we sent it out to patrol. When the unit discovered the body, they checked the picture. It's a match."

"Do you have any details, Curtis? Cause of death?"

"Not yet, but she didn't drown even though the fishermen found the body at the edge of the bay."

"The bay? Her body was found in the bay?" Detective Brody shot Elise a quick glance.

"Not in the bay, at the edge. Right over that small incline that borders the parking lot for the Golden Gate. That's why we know she didn't drown unless it was recent." His eyes shifted between Elise and the sketch artist, and he cleared his throat. "No bloating."

Elise covered her mouth and clenched her teeth.

Detective Brody stepped in front of her as if to shield her from the other detective's words and the image they'd already created in her head.

"We'll discuss the rest of this on the way."

Sergeant Curtis dipped his head. "Sorry, Ms. Duran. I'll ride with you, Brody."

"Are you going to be okay?" Detective Brody made a half turn toward her.

"I'm fine." Elise held up her hands. "I'm going straight to my friend's house after this."

"How will I reach you? We have to keep your phone."

"I should hope so." She shivered and rubbed her arms. "I'll pick up another phone today and contact you with the new number."

"Make sure you do. And Elise—" he pinned her with his dark gaze "—don't go back to your house."

She drew a cross over her heart. "I promise."

And that's the only thing she'd promise him right now.

Fifteen minutes later Elise sat in her car, her hands clutching the steering wheel. She could do this. She needed to know more, had a right to know more.

She rolled out of the parking garage and hung a left. She knew better than to follow Detective Brody's car. The guy seemed to be on high alert at all times. He'd notice one small hybrid following him to a crime scene.

Besides, she already knew the way. Hadn't her life almost ended in the exact same spot?

When she pulled into the parking lot for the bridge, she didn't have to worry about standing out. The tourist season was in high gear, and a trip to the Golden Gate Bridge was high on everyone's list.

A crowd of people had already formed at the edge of the lot where it led down to the gravel by the water. She stumbled from her car, and a brisk breeze cut her to the bone. She fished a sweater out of her backseat and put it on over her bulky cable knit. You could never have too many layers in San Francisco.

She scrambled from the car and tugged the sweater around her tighter, unrolling the sleeves so they hung over her hands. She shuffled up to the fringes of the crowd.

"What happened?" Elise stood on her tiptoes, not knowing what she hoped she would or wouldn't see.

A man looked over his shoulder. "There's a dead body down there."

The woman standing to her right clicked her tongue. "Is it a jumper?"

That's what the city workers had thought of her. Is that what this killer wanted everyone to believe? No. He wanted to shout his deeds from the rooftops. He wanted the distinction of impressing everyone with his cleverness or he never would've left that note for Brody.

The tall man in front of her snorted. "That's not a jumper this close to the shore. The current's too fast out there."

Elise ducked and shimmied between two of the curious onlookers. She zeroed in on Detective Brody's unmistakable form, his arm raised as if directing traffic.

Someone had covered the body with a sheet, securing the four corners against the wind that snatched at its edges. Frustrated in its efforts to pluck the sheet from the dead body, the wind found another outlet, puffing up the sheet so that it looked like a sail at full speed ahead.

But that girl wasn't going anywhere—ever.

Elise didn't know what she'd hoped to discover out here, but as soon as the other detective had burst into the interrogation room, she knew she had to see the crime scene for herself.

Had the killer intended this little patch of desolate shore as *her* final resting place? She turned her face to the right and gazed at the beach a short distance away where she'd scrambled into the water to save her life.

Had he killed this woman here or was this just his dumping ground?

She asked no one in particular. "Wh-who found her?"

The man with the broad shoulders turned sharply, bumping Elise's arm. "It's a woman? Who told you it was a woman?"

Elise grabbed the ponytail that whipped across her face. "Oh! I don't know. I guess I just assumed…"

The woman beside her grunted, "It's a woman. Count on it. Unless it's some drug hit or something. The cowards always go after the women."

The wail of a siren drew closer, causing the clutch of people to shift and sway.

Would they take her away now? Away from the prying eyes of this nosy group of people?

Elise felt protective toward the woman, and maybe that protectiveness sprang from guilt. Had this woman taken her place?

Detective Brody had pointed out that the killer could've taken that picture at any time. He was right. Chances are the killer hadn't found another victim after two in the morning when Elise had escaped.

Sergeant Curtis crunched across the gravel and faced the crowd. "Did anyone else see anything out here?"

Elise dropped her head and pulled the sweater up to her chin, not that he'd notice her after their brief encounter in the interrogation room.

People murmured and mumbled, but nobody stepped forward with any information.

Undeterred, Sergeant Curtis continued. "If anyone was here earlier, if anyone was taking any pictures, give us a call."

A few people began peeling away from the group as

the cops continued to scour the ground. A coroner's van had pulled up on the gravel, but still nobody made a move to retrieve the body.

They might be here all afternoon.

Elise spun away from the scene, her stomach rolling. Her presence here had served no purpose except to confirm how close her own brush with death had occurred to an actual death.

She reached into her purse for her cell phone before she remembered that her phone was in the possession of the SFPD with a picture of the dead woman below on it.

She meant what she told Brody. She wouldn't return to her house, not yet, especially with Oscar still out of town.

She tapped the arm of the woman next to her. "Can I borrow your phone for a minute? It's a local call."

"Sure." She dipped into the pocket of her sweatpants and pulled out a smartphone.

Elise tapped in Courtney's phone number.

"Hello?" Courtney's voice, low and seductive, purred over the line.

"Court? It's Elise."

"Elise?" The dulcet tones turned to a squeak. "Where are you calling from? I thought for sure you were Derrick from last night when I saw the unknown number."

"You wouldn't believe me if I told you."

"Are you okay? I texted you earlier but you didn't respond."

Elise took several steps away from the rubbernecking crowd, out of everyone's hearing. "All hell broke loose when I left you at the club last night."

Her friend paused for two beats. "Tell me you're okay right now before I have a full-fledged panic attack."

"I'm okay."

Courtney blew out a noisy sigh. "You scared me. What

do you mean all hell broke loose? Where are you and whose phone are you using?"

"After I left the club last night—" Elise closed her eyes and squeezed the phone "—I was attacked."

"Attacked? What are you talking about?"

Her friend's voice screeched over the phone and Elise pulled it away from her ear.

"Someone pretended to need help and when I went to help him, he knocked me on the head and stuffed me into his trunk."

Courtney's breath rasped over the phone. "Elise, you're joking. Tell me you're joking."

"I'm not joking, Courtney. I got away. I'm okay."

"How can you be okay after something like that? Where are you?" She sucked in a breath. "Oh, God, you're not in the hospital, are you?"

"Not anymore."

"Not anymore? Where *are* you? I'm coming to get you."

Elise switched the phone to her other hand and wiped her clammy palm against the seat of her jeans. "I was hoping you'd say that. There's more to the story."

A lot more to the story. She caught sight of Detective Brody's head as he clambered onto a rock, his tie dancing over his shoulder in the breeze.

"I don't need a ride, but I was hoping I could crash at your place for a night or two. Your brother's out of town again, and I don't feel like staying in the house alone."

"Absolutely. Do you have your car?"

"I do. Are you home now? I'll drive over."

"I'm not home. I'm shopping, and I was going to grab some lunch. Why don't you meet me for lunch?"

"I can do that. Where?"

"I'm at Union Square. How about Chinatown?"

"I don't know how I'm ever going to find parking there, but I'll give it a try. Han Ting's?"

"I'll meet you there at around one o'clock. Is that enough time for you?"

Elise agreed to the time and ended the call. She held the phone out to the woman. "Thank you."

"No problem."

"Any progress down there?" Elise stood on her tiptoes, but the scene looked much the same—people searching the ground, heads together conferring, and still the white sheet billowed in the wind.

"No. I'm going to continue my walk over the bridge. I suppose we'll be reading about this one in the newspaper."

"I hope so."

The woman's brow furrowed and Elise felt her cheeks warming. "I…I mean, I hope the cops keep the public informed about crime. Do they ever underreport this kind of stuff? You know, shove it under the carpet to give people a false sense of security and to keep the tourists coming?"

"I suppose." The woman cocked her head. "I read about another murder last month, a young woman. I hope we don't have some serial killer on the loose."

Elise didn't want to dash the stranger's hopes, so she sealed her lips. "I hope not. Anyway, thanks for the phone. Enjoy your walk."

She shoved her hands in the pockets of her sweater and watched the woman cross the parking lot and head toward the bridge's pedestrian walkway.

Elise had ventured across the bridge a few times since moving to the city. Round-trip was a good three-mile walk, and while she could use the exercise to clear her head, she had a lunch date with Courtney—not that she was looking forward to it.

She dreaded revealing the rest of last night's details to Courtney, except for meeting Detective Brody. She wanted her friend's take on the tall, muscular cop and his protective attitude toward her. Was his behavior normal for a homicide detective questioning a witness?

Normal or not, Elise had felt something click between them, or maybe that was just her desperately reaching out for a knight in shining armor. After Ty, she'd begun doubting the existence of those knights.

She dug in her purse for her keys, and then someone touched her shoulder. She spun around, dropping the keys and hugging her purse to her chest.

Sergeant Curtis faced her, his eyes narrowed and his arms across his barrel chest. "What are you doing here, Ms. Duran?"

Her gaze skittered over his shoulder to Detective Brody still clomping around the beach. "I just had to see for myself. That's not against the law, is it? All these other people are here."

"Of course not." He hunched his shoulders until his short neck disappeared completely. "But you're not like all these other people, are you?"

"I'm a curious looky-loo, just like them."

"Don't start doing your own investigating, Ms. Duran." He shook his stubby finger in her face. "Leave it to us. We'll tell you what you need to know."

Bending over, she swiped her keys up from the ground, hoping for a little composure. Sergeant Curtis's paternalistic tone caused a spiral of anger to shoot through her body. Why did men always think they knew what was best for her?

"Maybe I don't want to wait for information. That woman was on my phone. I have a right and a need to know what happened to her."

He took a step back and blinked. "Sorry. Just don't want you putting yourself in any danger."

"I get it." She waved him off and strode to her car, jabbing her thumb on the remote. He'd probably go and tell Detective Brody now.

And what if he did? She didn't owe Detective Brody anything, either.

As she rounded her car, a white square on her windshield caught her attention. She rolled her eyes. Perfect—a parking ticket.

She snatched the object from beneath her wiper, her eyebrows colliding over her nose. This was no ticket envelope. She unfolded the slip of paper and scanned the words.

The blood thundered in her ears as she crushed the paper in her fist, her gaze shifting wildly around the parking lot. Her dry mouth made forming words almost impossible.

She swallowed. She licked her lips. She tried again. She screamed.

"He's here. The killer's here."

Chapter Six

The woman's scream pierced through the air. The sound tore at Sean's insides. He jerked his head up and scanned the parking lot. A few of the vultures who had been circling the crime scene shifted their attention to a lone woman standing beside a car, waving her arms.

Standing beside a blue hybrid.

A long blond ponytail whipping across her face.

What the hell was Elise Duran doing here, and why the hell was she screaming?

The adrenaline pumped through his body, and his legs responded. He shot up the incline to the parking lot and sprinted across the asphalt.

Curtis had beaten him to it, but it didn't look as if he was having any luck getting a coherent response from Elise, still waving her arms around and talking gibberish.

"Elise! What's wrong? What are you doing here?"

She stumbled toward him, holding out a clenched fist, her face white. "He's here. He's here. The killer."

Adrenaline crashed through his body again before the first wave had even subsided, and he grabbed Elise's arms. "Where? Where is he?"

"Here." Her trembling fist prodded his chest. "He left this."

He had to practically pry open her frozen fingers to

get to the crumpled piece of paper she'd balled up in her clenched hand. He smoothed it out against the back of his hand and cursed.

Curtis hunched forward. "What is it, Brody? What's it say?"

"It says, 'Did you come to see my handiwork?'"

Curtis gurgled, his hand hovering over his weapon. "The SOB is here?"

"How long have you been away from your car, Elise? How much time did he have?"

Her head cranked back and forth. "I don't know. I mean, I've been here for about twenty minutes. I didn't notice anyone near my car. He's here. He was here."

"Maybe someone saw him." Sean shielded his eyes and tipped his head back to look at the lampposts. "Are there cameras on this part of the parking lot?"

"Nope. It's like our guy knows this area. No cameras where he dumped the body, either." Sergeant Curtis held out his hand for the note, and Sean extended it between two fingers even though he wanted to rip it to pieces.

Why had Elise come here anyway? He'd been worrying about her all the way to the crime scene, and she'd been right behind him.

"Where's Officer Jackson?"

"He's back at the crime scene, extending the yellow tape. Why?"

"I had him combing through the crowd earlier, asking questions, on the lookout for something just like this."

Elise's eyes popped open. "Really? You suspected the killer might be here?"

"A lot of times they stick around to prolong the thrill."

"That's taking a risk." She hugged herself and hunched farther into the big sweater she'd wrapped around her body.

"Our boy likes taking risks, doesn't he? He used your key to enter your house, sent a picture to your phone."

Her face crumpled. "Sent me *her* picture. Who is she, anyway?"

"We don't know yet." But the killer had sliced off her finger as a keepsake—something Elise didn't need to know.

Curtis held up the note. "Do you want me to put this in an evidence bag and track down Jackson to see if he saw anyone suspicious?"

"Yeah." Sean smacked the roof of Elise's car. "Ask him if he noticed anyone lurking around the parking lot, if he saw anyone near a blue hybrid."

Elise dragged a hand through her hair, loosening strands from her ponytail. "How did he find my car, Detective Brody? How did he know I was here?"

Despite her rigid posture, Elise looked ready to shatter into a million pieces. He tilted his chin toward the stone benches on the walkway to the visitor center. "Let's sit down over here. And you can call me Sean."

She turned and tripped over her own feet.

"Whoa." He took her arm to steady her and kept possession of it as they walked toward a bench.

She sat on the edge and crossed her legs, her head swiveling from side to side. "Do you think he's still here?"

"I think he's long gone. He must have a police scanner or he was watching the area, knew we'd gotten the call and rushed over to see the spectacle." He cleared his throat. "He must've seen you, Elise. Must've recognized you."

She closed her eyes and a breath shuddered through her body. "He knows my car because he saw it in my garage, so he looked for it."

"It must've increased his excitement tenfold to see you here."

She slammed a fist against the back of the bench. "Now I'm even more upset that I came out here. I don't want to give him any more satisfaction."

"Why did you follow us?"

"I didn't exactly follow you." She rubbed her hand, red from the sudden contact with the bench. "Sergeant Curtis had mentioned the location of the body, so I waited until you took off."

"That doesn't answer the question." The strands of her golden hair danced around her face, and his fingers itched to tuck them behind her ears. Instead he folded his arms and drove his fists into his biceps. "Why'd you come out here?"

"Are you seriously asking me that? Why wouldn't I come when I'm so involved?"

He sliced a hand through the air. "That's exactly why you need to stay out of this. Don't tempt this guy. You're the one who got away. Don't keep reminding him of that."

"You're right." She sniffled and pulled a tissue from her purse. "I guess I just had to see for myself. I feel...connected to this woman."

"I understand that, but just let us do our jobs. He's careless, addicted to the thrill. He wants the limelight. We'll bring him down." He touched her shoulder and then buried his hand in his pocket.

There was no doubt Elise needed protection, but she didn't need it from him. Death and darkness dominated his existence. Elise needed life and light and laughter. She needed to get out of this city.

"You're right." She lifted her shoulders and then blew out a sigh. "I just felt compelled to be here."

Sean narrowed his eyes as he turned his attention to the crime scene, where an officer was waving his arms at him. "Looks like they're flagging me down. What are you going to do?"

"I'm meeting my friend for lunch." She tugged at the sleeve of her sweater to reveal a watch. "And I'm going to be late."

"Where are you having lunch?"

She blinked. "Chinatown."

"It's going to be crazy over there. They're having a parade for the Dragon Boat Festival."

"I'm pretty sure my friend doesn't know that. Maybe I'll park elsewhere and hop on the Muni."

"I have a better idea. I'll put a call in to the station there and let them know you're going to park your car in the lot." He slipped the notebook from his pocket and jotted down the intersection for her.

"You can do that?"

"One of the perks of being a cop in the city." He pushed up from the bench and tucked the piece of paper in her hand. "I'll walk you back to your car. Just be aware of your surroundings. Keep an eye on your rearview mirror."

Her eyes widened. "You think he might follow me?"

"I think you need to be careful. Everyone should be aware of their surroundings."

"Especially me."

She clicked her remote, and he opened the car door for her, hanging on the frame. "You're going to get a phone and give me a call so I have the number?"

"I'll do that after lunch, and I have to at least drop by my place to pack a bag and get my school stuff together."

His gut knotted. "You still have to teach."

"One more week of school."

"Like I said, be aware of your surroundings."

She started her engine and snapped on her seat belt. "Thanks, Detective...Sean. Thanks for everything. I'll call when I get that phone."

His gaze trailed after her little car as it scooted out of the parking lot, and the knots in his gut tightened even more.

Of course she had to go to work and see her friends and live her life. He couldn't follow her around the city.

Even though he wanted to.

ELISE GLIDED INTO a parking stall at the Central Division and gave her rearview mirror one last glance. If anyone had followed her here, he'd have to be a ninja. She'd taken so many twists and turns to avoid the areas blocked off for the parade route, she would've noticed someone on her tail taking the exact same route.

She flipped up the mirror cover on the visor and dashed some color across her lips. She needed all the artificial brightening she could handle after that shock at the bridge.

He'd spotted her. Knew her car. Maybe he'd been watching her.

She smacked the visor against the roof of the car. He was too cocky. Detective Brody—Sean—was right. The killer would trip up sooner rather than later with his attitude of invincibility.

"Sean." Just saying his name made her feel more at ease. He'd even secured a parking space for her in the middle of Chinatown on a parade day. Now, there was a man you could count on—not like Ty, filled with secrets, lies and betrayals.

She slipped out of the car and walked down the ramp to the sidewalk. Red and gold banners festooned lampposts and flapped in the breeze. Elise navigated between colorful lawn chairs and blankets lining the sidewalks. She sniffed the air filled with the scents of incense, spices and fried food. A pack of kids jostled her as they ran down the sidewalk clutching flags with red dragons emblazoned upon them. Their grandparents shuffled in their wake, smiling and nodding at Elise.

She ducked into the dark confines of Han Ting and surveyed the packed dining room. She and Courtney would be lucky to find a table.

"Elise!"

Elise peered across the room at Courtney bobbing up from her seat and waving in her direction. She wound through the tables and gave her friend a one-armed hug before sitting down.

"How in the world did you get a table? Did you even know that the Dragon Boat Parade was going on today?"

Courtney flicked her perfectly manicured fingers. "Duh. I grew up in Chinatown, remember? I know what today is."

"And how did you manage to snag a table? It's wall-to-wall people in here."

"My auntie's family owns Han Ting. Technically, she's not my aunt, but her family and my mom's family lived next door to each other in the old neighborhood."

"First a prime parking spot, and then the best table in the house at Han Ting. It pays to know people in high places."

"You got a parking spot?"

"It's a long story." Elise dropped a napkin in her lap and poured herself some tea from the ornate pot.

"Stop stalling and tell me what happened after you left me." Courtney tapped her cup and Elise filled it with the fragrant green tea.

As Elise relayed the details of the frightening episode, Courtney's lipsticked mouth formed a perfect O and she clutched her napkin to her chest.

"Oh, my God, you are so amazing."

"Amazing? I wasn't even thinking straight. I just knew I had to get out of that trunk. I was also mad at myself for falling prey to his broken-arm scam."

Elise held her breath, waiting for Courtney to agree with her. *She* never would've fallen for that ruse.

"Are you kidding?" Courtney dropped her napkin and gulped the rest of her tea. "Anybody would've done the same thing. He had a cast on. Who would go to those lengths?"

"I guess it's not the first time a serial killer has used that method."

"Serial killer?" Courtney covered her mouth when the waiter approached the table. She rattled off their order in Mandarin, and when the waiter left she focused her bright eyes on Elise again.

"How do you know this is a serial killer and not some random nut?"

Elise folded her hands around the warm cup. "Because he killed again."

"How do you know?"

Elise explained how the runner found her purse and phone and how the killer had sent the picture of his next victim. "Then when I was at the police station working with the sketch artist, a call came in that someone had found the woman's body."

"Elise, this is too creepy." She grabbed Elise's wrist, her nails digging into her skin. "You can't stay at the house, especially with Oscar gone."

"That's where you come in, if it's okay."

"Of course it's okay."

The waiter rolled up a cart with enough steaming plates to feed the Hun army. When he transferred all the dishes to the table, Elise dumped a mound of sticky white rice onto her plate.

As Elise ladled three different entrees onto her plate, she wondered whether or not she should tell Courtney about the note on her windshield.

She glanced at her friend dabbing a spot of red sauce at the corner of her mouth with a napkin and decided against it. She'd shocked Courtney enough for one sunny afternoon. She didn't need to hear the rest of the frightening details.

"Do they know how the woman died or how long she'd been there?"

"Change of subject, please. I want to enjoy my lunch."

"You don't have to tell *me* twice." Courtney stabbed a shrimp and shook it at Elise. "Here's a subject change for you—how hot is this Detective Brody who's following you around and scoring you parking places all over the city?"

Elise's face got warmer than the kung pao chicken. "Who said he was hot?"

Courtney snorted. "You did. Every time you mentioned his name and or his heroic deeds, you got all dreamy-eyed."

"That's ridiculous." Elise plucked the shrimp from Courtney's fork and popped it into her mouth.

"Don't forget, I read body language for a living, and you have one of those faces that show all your emotions—must be a Montana thing."

"Okay, I succumb to your superior understanding. Detective Sean Brody is hot—tall, dark and handsome."

Courtney held out her fist for a bump. "Well, all right. That's one silver lining to a very scary night."

"And you? Who's Derrick, and did he ever call you?"

"Derrick is that fine African-American who bought us that second round of drinks."

"Bought *you* a second round. I just had one, remember?"

"Whatever. After you left, we danced the rest of the night."

"He seemed like a nice guy, but kind of a player."

"Okay, not every guy is a player like your Montana cowboy. Look at the luscious Detective Brody. I'll bet he's not a player."

She shrugged. "Doesn't seem like it, but I don't know much about him."

Courtney's phone buzzed, and as she checked the display, a crease formed between her eyebrows. "Client. I need to take this."

"Do you want to take some of this food to go?"

"Sure. Have them pack it up." Courtney scooted back her chair, already punching in her client's number.

She might be a party girl on the surface, but as a therapist Courtney was committed to her clients. She'd drop everything at a moment's notice to see them and talk them through some crisis.

Elise asked for some to-go boxes and was scooping the food into the little white cartons when Courtney returned to the table.

Courtney unhooked her purse from the back of her chair. "I'm so sorry. I'm going to have to run out on you and meet my client at my office—emergency. Can you take the food? You can go straight to my place. I'll give you the key."

She reached for her wallet, but Elise held up her hand. "I'll get lunch. After all, I'm going to be your guest for the next few days."

"Longer if you need it." She waved to an old Chinese woman stationed by the door. "Auntie Lu, come and say hello to my friend."

Elise stood up and exchanged a quick hug with her friend, who then kissed Auntie Lu's pale cheek on her way out of the restaurant.

The old woman placed a hand on Elise's arm. "Sit."

Elise sat down and Auntie Lu arranged herself in the chair across from her.

"Courtney busy girl."

"Courtney is a good friend." Elise pulled some bills from her wallet and dropped them onto the check tray. "How long has your family owned this restaurant?"

"Many years. You going to watch the parade today? Starting soon."

"I am."

Auntie Lu tapped Elise's teacup. "You have leaves. Do you want me to read your tea leaves?"

"Can you do that?"

"Ancient practice." She winked at Elise and slid the cup in front of her, wrapping her gnarled hands with their painted nails and heavy rings around it.

Auntie Lu studied the bottom of the cup, and the smile she'd been wearing faded. Then she pushed the cup away. "Silly."

A wisp of fear trailed across Elise's flesh. "What is it? What did you see in there?"

Auntie Lu spread her crooked fingers. "Nothing. I lost my touch."

She eased from the chair, patted Elise's shoulder and shuffled back to her stool by the door, where she stared onto the street through the window.

Elise tipped the cup and squinted at the residue swimming in the bottom. Then she splashed a little more tea into the cup and gulped it, leaves and all. "That takes care of that fortune."

She dropped her wallet back into her purse, hitched it over her shoulder and hung the plastic bag of food over her wrist. She smiled and nodded at Auntie Lu by the entrance and grabbed the door handle.

Auntie Lu's seemingly frail hand gripped Elise's elbow in a vise. Elise looked into her dark, gleaming eyes.

Auntie Lu whispered, "Be careful."

For a second, Elise thought she'd imagined the entire exchange as Auntie Lu's grip turned into a light squeeze and she smiled and nodded. "Goodbye, Ming Na friend."

Elise knew Ming Na was Courtney's middle name, so she smiled back and pushed out of the suddenly oppressive darkness of the restaurant into the sunshine.

The pedestrian traffic on the sidewalk had doubled since lunch. Elbows and shoulders bumped as people jostled for position on the sidewalk facing the parade route.

Elise threaded through the crowd, looking for a gap

she could squeeze through to get a clear view of the festivities. She darted across the street and then backtracked toward Han Ting.

Spying daylight, she scooted through two people and popped up behind a boy and a girl wiggling with excitement.

The acrobats led the parade, clutching sticks with colorful streamers on the end that created a kaleidoscope of hues as they leaped and tumbled. A float decorated with flowers sailed past, cradling the royal court of Dragon Boat princesses and their queen, all doing the parade wave and smiling.

A few firecrackers popped and the kids in front of her squealed as Elise jumped, clutching her purse.

A Boy Scout troop marched by and the fresh, innocent faces of the kids calmed her nerves.

Nerves? When had she started feeling anxious? The press of people didn't bother her; even after coming from the wide-open spaces of Montana, Elise had reveled in the crowds and excitement of the city.

It must have been the noise from the firecrackers that had set her teeth on edge. Or the warning from Auntie Lu.

Ridiculous. She already knew to be careful after her encounter with a killer. Auntie Lu wasn't telling her something she didn't already have imprinted on her brain, and Auntie Lu probably issued that warning to all young women.

Standing on her tiptoes, Elise clapped loudly and whistled as the winner of the boat race passed by displaying his victorious boat. The kids in front of her covered their ears. She got the attention of her kindergartners by whistling—worked every time.

With each passing parade participant, the people behind her pressed in closer and closer. She leaned back, not wanting to push the children into the street. By now she could barely move, barely turn her head.

The dragon float made its appearance, its head shaggy with crepe paper tilting back and forth to the delight of the crowd, which surged forward. Elise hooked her arms around the kids' shoulders to protect them.

The dragon undulated forward, its body twisting this way and that way. Another round of firecrackers exploded so close Elise could smell the acrid gunpowder.

A sharp pain stabbed her thigh and she lurched forward, knocking the kids off the curb.

"I'm so sorry."

They giggled as she tried to pull them back onto the sidewalk. Elise couldn't even drop her arms to her sides to feel her leg. Someone must've had something sharp in a purse or pocket, or maybe a little kid had jabbed her with some trinket from the knickknack shops that lined the streets.

The last flick of the dragon's tail signaled the end of the parade, and people began to shuffle away, giving everyone a little more breathing room.

"Are you guys okay?" Elise finally had room to bend forward and check on the kids.

They nodded and scampered away.

Elise trailed her hand down the back of her thigh toward the sore spot. The material of her jeans gaped open, and she drew her brows over her nose.

What the heck had gouged her?

Her fingers probed the ripped denim and her skin beneath, and she gasped as they met moisture. She snatched her hand away and brought it in front of her face.

Her stomach lurched and a scream ripped from her throat. The people milling around her backed away, creating a ring of space around her.

She dragged her gaze away from her hand and tried to

focus on the faces swimming before her. Only one face stood out—Auntie Lu's as she hovered in the doorway of her restaurant, her dark eyes sharp amid the lines of age.

Elise swallowed and gasped to no one and everyone. "I've been stabbed."

Chapter Seven

The woman had been stabbed, her throat slit.

Sean massaged his temples. So much blood. Had that been the fate this maniac had intended for Elise?

He pounded his fist on his desk, and the pencils in the holder jumped and rattled. He slid one between his fingers and rat-tatted it on the blotter.

Elise hadn't called him yet with her phone number. He checked his watch. She and her friend had a lot to talk about over lunch, and the Dragon Boat Parade was probably still going on.

He ran his finger over the receiver of his desk phone. He could call Central Station to see if her car was still parked in the lot.

As if by magic, the phone rang beneath his hand, and he wrapped his fingers around the receiver. "Brody, homicide."

"Detective Brody, this is Officer Yin with Central. We have a situation here with one of your witnesses, Elise Duran. She requested that we call you."

"A situation?" Sean's pulse picked up speed.

"Someone stabbed her on the parade route."

The pencil in Sean's other hand snapped. "Is she all right?"

She had to be. She'd asked for him.

"The wound just broke the skin. She's okay, but understandably upset. We've got an ambulance on the scene, but she doesn't want to go the hospital and insisted we call you first."

"Does she need to go the hospital?" Sean had already grabbed his jacket from the back of his chair and swept his keys into his pocket.

Elise needed him.

"My guess is she's going to need stitches."

"Get her in that ambulance and tell her I'll meet her at the hospital. And I'm gonna want your report."

"You got it."

For the second time in as many days, Sean raced to the hospital to see Elise—only this time it was much more personal.

When he got to the emergency room, he found her sitting on an examination table, her legs swinging and hospital paper wrapped around her waist.

She jerked her head up at his approach. "Can you believe this? He got to me. I swear I wasn't followed."

In two steps he was at her side. "Tell me what happened."

"I was standing in a big crowd of people watching the parade. When the dragon float passed by, everyone surged forward. I could barely breathe. I was just trying to keep my balance when I felt a sharp pain in my thigh."

She rolled onto the side of her hip and pointed to a bandage on the back of her leg.

Sean flinched at the spot of blood forming in the center of the white gauze bandage. It was not as if he hadn't seen his share of blood. Hadn't he just left a bloodbath on the shore of the bay? Seeing Elise injured made his blood boil. She'd endured enough already.

How had he gotten to her?

She continued. "When the crowd cleared, I reached

down to feel the sore spot and found sliced jeans and blood instead."

"Did anyone see anything? Notice anybody?"

"Not that I know of." She twisted her lips. "I screamed bloody murder, and I think that scared everyone away. The cops asked around, but nobody noticed anything."

"Cameras in the area?" He knew that some cameras were stationed in Chinatown, but closer to the banks on the edge of the area.

She shrugged and her eyes widened. "How'd he find me, Sean? I'm sure nobody followed me. I kept my eyes glued to that rearview mirror."

"Maybe this was just a random attack. Were there any other reports of violence along the parade route?"

"You don't believe that. I can tell by your voice you don't believe it. You don't have to try to make me feel better."

Oh, but he did. He wanted to run his hands across the smooth skin of her face and brush away all the pain and fear.

"Just trying to look at all possibilities."

A doctor poked her head into the room. "Are you Elise's husband?"

"I'm Detective Brody, SFPD Homicide."

The doctor's brows shot up. "Homicide?"

"We think this attack is related to a murder. Is Elise going to be okay?"

"She'll be fine. We cleaned the wound and I'm going to put in a few stitches. You can wait in the hallway or the waiting room."

"I want him to stay…if he wants to."

"I'm not going anywhere." He shouldn't have made a promise he couldn't keep. He couldn't be Elise's round-the-clock bodyguard and protector—but the wobbly smile she'd just aimed at him made him want to try.

The doctor snapped on a pair of gloves, and the nurse wheeled a cart of instruments next to the cot.

"Lie down on your stomach and we'll get this stitched right up."

The paper on the table crinkled as Elise scooted back and rolled to her stomach.

Sean sat in a plastic chair in the corner while the doctor and nurse went to work. The killer must've followed Elise from the bridge parking lot and she hadn't noticed. That meant he'd been lurking around waiting for her. Someone that bold would make a mistake sooner or later.

And if this guy wanted to continue playing games with him, he'd have the pleasure of bringing him down.

"Try not to get it wet." The doctor was peeling off her gloves. "And you should be fine."

Fifteen minutes later, Sean was escorting Elise out of the hospital. "I'm assuming your car's still parked in Chinatown."

"It's still at the station." She turned and wedged her back against his car. "Why did he do it? Why did he come after me again if he wasn't planning to kill me?"

"I think it's obvious."

"Why didn't he take the opportunity to kill me?"

"In the middle of Chinatown? That would've been a little more noticeable. He sliced your leg in the crowd, knowing you might not register the pain right away or wouldn't immediately identify what had happened. Then he made his getaway."

"But why did he bother? Why take that chance if he wasn't going to finish the job he'd started last night?"

"He's toying with you, Elise. He's sending you the message that he can get to you."

She shrugged off the car and yanked the door open before he could reach for it. "Let him try."

Sean chewed the inside of his cheek as he went around

to the driver's side of his car. He understood Elise's anger, but a healthy dose of fear wasn't necessarily a bad thing.

He started the car. "I didn't ask, but I take it your friend wasn't with you at the time of the attack?"

"She had an emergency with a client—she's a therapist."

"I hope you asked if you could stay at her place."

Elise reached into the side pocket of her purse and dangled a key ring from her finger. "I'm all set, but I have to go back to my place to pack a bag and get my stuff for school."

"Does your friend live closer to you or closer to Chinatown?"

"Closer to Chinatown. Why?"

"How about if I drive you to your place first and then take you to your car at the station?"

"Are you a cop or a chauffeur?"

"Sometimes I ask myself the same question."

She tapped his arm. "No, really, I don't want to put you out."

"No problem." Problem? Sean was reluctant to let her out of his sight. If she thought she'd been looking out for a tail when she'd left the bridge and this guy managed to follow her anyway, he must be good.

Elise's temporary digs had better be secure, or he didn't think he'd be able to leave her. She'd gotten under his skin, not that he hadn't felt protective about witnesses before. That was in his DNA. It was in the Brody DNA.

Something about Elise pushed all his buttons. Her prettiness had a different quality from the rest of the drop-dead-gorgeous women in the city. Her fresh face and quick smile had an irresistible openness—irresistible to him, anyway.

He had to admit that his attraction to her stemmed, in part, to her ignorance about him, about his family. About the dark cloud that hung over his head. Couldn't she see it following him around?

When they got to her house, he stepped in front of her at the door. "Let me check it out first."

He did a quick sweep of the small house, including the bathroom, where the note on the mirror still mocked him. "All clear."

"I figured that."

Crossing his arms, he blocked her entrance into the living room. "Don't let down your guard, Elise. He's out there. He's watching you. He's already proved that."

"You're right." She swept past him. "I just don't like the idea of this guy controlling my life. I don't want anyone controlling my life."

"I get it, but you still need to be careful."

"I know." She banged a few cupboard doors in the kitchen and emerged holding a bowl and a carton of milk. "I'd better leave something for Straycat."

She tucked the milk in the crook of her arm as she slid open the door to the patio. The dish clinked as she set it down on the porch. "Straycat!"

"Does he actually come to that name?"

"No, he's very independent."

"I guess he doesn't want anyone controlling his life, either."

She jerked her head up and studied his face. Then she opened her mouth, snapped it shut and stepped into the room. "I'm going to throw some things in a bag. Would you like something to drink or eat? A banana?"

"Banana?"

"I just bought a bunch and I don't want them to go to waste if I have to leave them for several days."

"I'll take one." He walked into the kitchen and snapped a banana from the bunch. Peeling it, he strolled to Elise's room, where she was pulling clothes from a hanger and stuffing them into a suitcase, and he leaned against the doorjamb.

"How's your leg feeling?"

Without looking up from her task, she replied, "Fine."

"Do you need me to do anything? Check your locks? Leave a lamp on?"

She stood back from the overflowing suitcase, hands on her hips. "You like to help, don't you?"

Heat crawled up his neck and he took a big bite of the banana. Chewing allowed him to avoid the question. He swallowed and shrugged. "I'm a cop. That's what we do."

"Ah, but which came first?" She plunged her hands into the suitcase to flatten the clothes. "Did your desire to help people encourage you to become a cop, or once you became a cop did you just naturally develop that trait?"

He swung the banana peel back and forth. "You know, I never analyzed it. The career runs in the family."

"Really?"

"My brothers are all in law enforcement."

"How many brothers do you have?"

"Three."

"That's a coincidence. I have three brothers, too."

Great. He needed to change this subject. If he spent much more time in Elise's presence, he'd be revealing all his secrets. Secrets better kept to himself.

He backed out of the room, waving the banana peel. "I'm going to toss this."

When he returned to the bedroom, he took up his position at the door. "So, what do your brothers do?"

"Make my life miserable." She leaned on the suitcase with one hand and used the other to yank at the zipper.

Sean took two steps into the room, hunched over and held the suitcase down while she zipped it. "Mine can do that, too."

Still bent over the suitcase, she turned suddenly and her golden hair brushed his arm. "Nice to see a human side to you, Detective."

He didn't move an inch. The ends of her ponytail tickled his arm. The pulse in her throat beat out waves of her floral perfume. Her bright blue eyes sparkled with curiosity and humor.

Time seemed to freeze for a few seconds, and in those few seconds he had an overwhelming urge to take possession of her plump lips. To lose himself in the rush of senses that her presence stirred in him. To find out what it felt like to taste sunshine.

The over-the-top thoughts running through his mind must've shown on his face.

Her eyes widened and her lips parted as she lodged the tip of her tongue in the corner of her mouth.

He didn't need a body language expert to tell him what her response meant. Hell, he *was* a body language expert. If he kissed her now, he'd meet no resistance.

He smacked his palms on the lid of the suitcase and straightened to his full height, feeling as if he were emerging from a spell. "School stuff?"

"What?" Elise blinked her eyes.

"I can take your suitcase out to the car while you get your school materials."

"Oh, yeah. I keep them all together in a bag." She swiveled her head from side to side as if lost in her own house.

Sean hoisted the suitcase from the bed, pulled out the handle and stated the obvious. "I'll take this."

She nodded and scooted past him into the living room to retrieve her school bag.

Sean loaded the suitcase in the car and returned to the house.

Elise dropped her school bag at his feet. "I forgot my shampoo and stuff. I'll dump it in another bag."

She darted for the hallway, and Sean followed. As she plucked items from her medicine chest and a shower caddy,

Sean pointed to the mirror. "Do you want me to clean that up? We got all the evidence we're going to get from it."

"Go ahead. It's your message." She hitched the bag over her shoulder and tilted her head. "Did you ever figure out what it meant?"

"He hasn't contacted me again. Probably just a jab at law enforcement."

He'd figured the guy probably knew his history and was taunting him. Wouldn't be the first time.

"There's a roll of paper towels on the counter and window cleaner under the sink in the kitchen."

The lipstick smeared the mirror as he swept damp paper towels across it. A few more swipes and the words disappeared. If only he could erase them from his mind as easily.

Elise hovered at the bathroom door. "Ready? I have everything."

"Let's go." He crumpled the used paper towels in his hand and dropped them into the kitchen trash and replaced the glass cleaner under the sink.

He loaded her remaining bags in the trunk of his car and took off for what he hoped would be her safe house for a while.

They wended their way through the city streets as the late-afternoon sun streamed through the buildings and glinted off the water that made an occasional appearance when they crested a hill.

Sean pulled into the lot at the Central Station in Chinatown, where Elise's hybrid huddled between two patrol cars. If the killer had followed her here, where had he parked? Spaces were at a premium and he wouldn't have wanted to risk a parking ticket, which could be traced.

Maybe he'd watched from his car as she went into the restaurant and then figured he'd have time to park in a public lot near Union Square and pick up her trail on foot when she'd finished lunch. However he'd done it, the guy was no amateur.

Had he killed before somewhere else and then taken his sick proclivities on the road to terrorize a new city?

He pulled behind Elise's car, leaving the engine running.

She opened the door and placed one foot on the ground. "Aren't you going to transfer my bags from your car to mine?"

"I told you. I'm following you over. I'll bring your bags in for you when we get there."

She rattled off her friend's address. "In case I lose you on the way."

He whistled. "Nice neighborhood."

"Family money. Their parents owned a lot of properties here, including that house where I live."

"Good. That's a safe part of town."

He followed Elise's car. She drove so slowly, there's no way she could lose him—and probably no way she could've avoided being tailed by her stalker, no matter what she believed.

She pulled in front of a modern building, supported by gleaming white pillars. She pointed out her car window at a driveway that sloped down toward a wrought-iron gate.

Sean made a U-turn and parked in front of the condo complex while Elise rolled into the parking garage. He popped the trunk and gathered Elise's two bags over one shoulder and settled her suitcase on its wheels.

"I can take one of those." Elise had appeared on a walkway next to the driveway.

"I got 'em. Lead the way." He followed her up the marble tile steps, and she used her friend's key to open the front door. "Is your friend going to be home?"

"I have no idea."

They went to the second floor and Elise stopped at one

of just three doors on the hallway. She knocked first, listened and then unlocked the door.

The decor of the condo almost blinded him—modern, tasteful and white. He preferred Elise's jumble of colorful styles.

She called out, "Courtney?"

There was an upstairs as well, and Elise stood at the foot of the staircase, her hand resting on the chrome banister.

"I guess she's not home yet."

Sean parked her suitcase in a corner and piled her other two bags on top of it. "I'll stick around until she gets here."

Elise spun around and plopped down on the second step of the staircase. "Did you find out anything about the woman on my phone?"

"Her name's Katie Duncan, twenty-five years old."

"Duncan? That's weird."

"Do you know the name?"

"Duncan, Duran—maybe he's going through the phone book." She snapped her fingers. "What was the name of the other woman? The one found at the Presidio?"

"Carlson."

Her eyes popped. "C, D."

"Are you in the phone book?" Sean's hand tightened on the banister. Of course, he'd noticed the similarity between Elise's and Katie's names, but who used phone books anymore?

"No, I'm not. I suppose it's just a coincidence, but maybe he's looking at some alphabetical list of something."

Pain needled the back of his neck and he clasped it, rolling his head.

"Are you okay?"

"Headache." He dropped to the bottom step and leaned against the wall. "Katie wasn't a teacher, so it's not some alphabetical list of teachers."

"What *did* she do?"

"She was a legal secretary."

"Had she ever been to the Speakeasy, like me?"

"We're looking into it." He leveled a finger at her. "You're becoming a good detective."

"I have a vested interest in seeing Katie's, and maybe the Carlson woman's, killer nailed. I don't want to live in fear. He may not know where I'm staying now, but he knows my name. Who knows what kind of info he can get on me?"

A key scraped in the lock and the front door swung open. Sean jumped to his feet as a young Asian woman stumbled into the entryway loaded down with shopping bags.

She stopped when she saw them and dropped half the bags. "You scared the spit out of me!"

"Sorry." Elise squeezed past him on the stairs and hugged her friend, bags and all. "Courtney, this is Detective Sean Brody. Sean, this is Courtney Chu."

Courtney dropped the rest of her bags and stuck out her hand. "Nice to meet you."

She arched an eyebrow at Elise. "Is he moving in, too?"

"N-no. He, well, he followed me here. There was an incident at the Dragon Boat Parade."

"What?" Courtney gripped Elise's shoulders.

"I was attacked."

Courtney let out a yelp and then herded Elise to her spotless living room and sat her down.

Elise told her the story while Courtney alternately gasped, cursed and covered her mouth with her hand.

"Elise, this is crazy." She turned on Sean, her black hair whipping across her face. "What are you doing to catch this guy?"

"Everything we can." He pulled the sketch Elise had helped create out of his pocket and smoothed out the creases. "Here he is. You didn't notice him in the club that night, did you? You didn't notice anyone watching Elise?"

"Look at her." She jerked her thumb at Elise. "She's gorgeous. Of course I noticed guys watching her, but not this nut job."

Sean's phone buzzed in his pocket and he pulled it out, glancing at the display. "It's the station. I'm going to take this and then I'll get out of your way."

He rose from the chair and wandered into the kitchen as Elise and her friend continued their excited chatter.

"Brody."

"Brody, it's Curtis. You'd better get down here."

Sean's heart pounded and the blood thudded in his ears. "What's up?"

"That dead girl we found today? Katie Duncan?"

"Yeah?" With his mouth suddenly gone dry, Sean could barely form the word.

"Her killer sent you a message."

"What'd it say?" Sean clenched his jaw where a muscle twitched erratically.

"It's not so much what he said, dude, as what he sent."

Sean spat out an expletive. "Just tell me."

"He sent you a finger, Brody. Katie Duncan's severed finger."

Chapter Eight

Only half listening to Courtney's exclamations, Elise directed her gaze at Sean clutching his cell phone to his ear. With his back turned toward her, she couldn't see his face but his shoulders had a rigid set and his white knuckles made it look as if he could crush that phone with one hand.

Courtney snapped her fingers. "Earth to Elise."

"Sorry. What were you saying?"

"Never mind." Courtney turned her head to look at Sean. "Not as important as *some* things."

Sean ended the call and took a few steps into the room, his face stern and white. "Duty calls. I gotta go back to the station. Take care of that leg, and don't forget to pick up a phone and give me the number."

"My leg's fine, and I'll get that phone." Elise pushed up from the sofa. "Hold on, I'll see you out."

Courtney waved. "Bye, nice to meet you. Maybe we'll see each other again."

Elise stepped into the hallway with him and pulled the door shut. "Is everything okay?"

He relaxed his jaw enough to speak. "Everything's fine, except we have a diabolical killer loose in the city."

"What was the call about?"

"Murder and mayhem—just an ordinary day on the job. That's my life, Elise, and you don't need to hear about it."

Did he think she couldn't handle reality? She grabbed his arm and his biceps felt like granite. "You can tell me. You don't have to push me away."

He cupped her face in one large hand and stroked his thumb across her cheek. "Yes, I do."

His touch belied his words, and his proximity had her breath coming in short spurts. "But I don't want you to."

The harsh kiss he pressed against her mouth came so suddenly, it took her breath way. Just as quickly it ended and he turned on his heel and disappeared into the stairwell.

Elise put two fingers to her bruised lips and backed into Courtney's condo.

"Sean Brody is one hot detective." Courtney's words sang out amid the banging of cupboard doors and pots and pans.

Closing her eyes, Elise took a deep breath and then turned and joined her friend in the kitchen. "Good-looking guy, but still a cop."

Courtney dropped a package of pasta on the countertop. "Are cops off-limits for some reason?"

"Oh, you know." Elise waved her hand in the air. "Control issues."

"Small price to pay, girl. And I'd say you're the one with control issues. He's obviously interested."

"Why do you say that?" Courtney involuntarily brushed the tips of her fingers against her chin where Sean's stubble had scratched her.

"I'm a therapist, remember? I'm trained to read people, even people as zipped up as Detective Brody."

"Do you think he's zipped up?"

Courtney bit her lip as she filled a pot with water. "He holds himself very still, holds his emotions in check. But, come on. What cop goes out of his way to escort a witness around? Even a cute little girl-next-door like you?"

"I think he's just doing his job and he's thorough." Elise tugged on the ends of Courtney's hair. "How was your client this afternoon?"

"I had to talk her down from a ledge, but she was okay."

"Not literally?"

"An emotional ledge." Courtney presented a bottle of wine to Elise, label out. "I think you need a little vino tonight."

"I think you're right." She took the bottle from Courtney and held out her hand. "Corkscrew."

Elise poured two glasses of wine and sidled next to Courtney at the sink. "Let me make the salad since you're sacrificing your Saturday night to stay in with me, and don't even deny it. Did Derrick ever call?"

"He texted me. We'll probably get together sometime this week. He's out of town this weekend." She stirred the pasta into the bubbling water as steam rose to the ceiling.

They worked side by side in the kitchen for several minutes, and Elise soaked in the normalcy. She had a hard time grasping the events of the past twenty-four hours. She'd been abducted, had escaped and had been attacked again—and she'd met Sean Brody. This time yesterday, she'd been getting ready to go out with Courtney.

As her friend dumped the pasta into a colander in the sink, Elise carried the salad to the table. "Do you mind if I turn on the local evening news?"

"Really? I don't mind but it's the last thing I thought you'd want to watch." Courtney wiped her hands on a dish towel and retrieved the remote from the coffee table in the living room.

They settled at the kitchen table, and the smell of the garlic mingled with the hint of fennel in the sausage to make Elise's mouth water. She took a sip of red wine, lolling it on her tongue before she swallowed.

Then she clicked on the TV and muted the sound. She

kept her eye on the commercials as she stabbed a couple of rigatoni with her fork. "Yummy. You'll have to give me..."

A wind-blown reporter was speaking into a mic, a shot of the Golden Gate Bridge behind him. Elise pointed the remote at the TV and stabbed at the volume button.

"...found this morning by a couple of fishermen." The reporter backed up to the yellow crime tape flapping in the breeze. "Detective? Detective? Ray Lopez, KFGG News. Can you tell us anything about the victim? Does this murder have anything to do with the transient murders in the Tenderloin or that woman found near the Presidio?"

Sean's profile looked carved from stone. He barely moved his lips when he said, "No comment at this time."

"What about the attack on the woman last night? Is this related, Detective?"

"No comment." Sean turned his back on the reporter and bent his head to talk with one of the cops on the scene.

"There you have it, Jan. The police are keeping tight-lipped about this one, but the women of this city want to know. Is it safe to go out at night?"

The anchor and the reporter prattled on for several more seconds before Elise muted the TV again. "I guess my story's already out there."

"Sounds like it." Courtney raised her glass and swirled the contents. "But if those vultures ever get your name, make sure you follow Brody's example. No comment. They'll tear you apart."

"The last thing I need is publicity."

Courtney ran her fingertip along the rim of her glass. "Detective Brody sounds familiar to me. Did he write a book or something? Or maybe he was involved in a big case."

"If so, it was before my time here."

"Brody, Brody." Courtney's brow furrowed. "He must've been in the news."

"Probably. More wine?"

"Sure. It's Saturday night. Why not live it up?"

"You don't have to babysit. My leg feels fine, and I'll probably just go to bed early."

Courtney tossed back the last of her wine and held out her glass to Elise. "No problem. I'm tired from last night anyway. Besides, what did that reporter say? Is it even safe to go out at night?"

Elise took the glass by the stem and padded back to the kitchen, running her tongue along her lower lip. Apparently, it wasn't even safe for her to go out in broad daylight. At least not without the protection of Detective Sean Brody.

And how long could that last?

SEAN STARED AT the severed finger with the blue nail polish nestled in cotton. The package in which it had been delivered had come addressed to SFPD—Homicide. But when the front desk opened the box, they'd found the gruesome souvenir with a note pasted in the lid of the box: *This finger is pointing at you, Brody.*

"What does it mean, Brody?" Captain Williams's dark eyes drilled him. "This along with the note at the escaped victim's house make it clear that this is the same guy—and for some reason he's got it in for you."

"I'm supposed to know why?" Sean closed the lid on the finger and pushed it across the captain's desk. "Has the lab tested the finger yet?"

"Not yet, but who else's could it be?" Captain Williams steepled his own fingers and peered at Sean over the pinnacle. "I don't like this communication business, Brody."

Sean pinched the bridge of his nose. "That makes two of us."

"We took a risk bringing you into homicide, a risk I never regretted for one minute based on your performance."

"Until now?" Sean's fingers curled around the arms of the chair.

"Do you really think this killer would be sending you messages and uh…other gifts if not for your father?"

"Serial killers send messages to homicide detectives. It happens all the time."

Williams snorted. "Happens all the time in movies and TV. You and I both know it's not so common in real life."

"What do you want from me, Captain? I'm not going to hide under a rock. I have a murder and an attempted murder to solve, and if this guy wants to give me clues, so be it. I'll take whatever I can get."

"All right. I just hope some hotshot reporter doesn't start snooping around and dredging up old news. The department doesn't need it."

"Neither do I, sir."

"Now, do your job and—" he waved one hand over the box on his desk "—take this thing with you."

Sean picked up the box and walked out of the captain's office, his back stiff and his chin held high. If just one person mentioned his father, he'd deck 'em.

He strode down the hallway, holding the box in front of him, daring anyone to make a comment. Nobody even seemed to notice what he was holding.

Blowing out a breath, he poked his head into the lab. "I think you guys are waiting for a finger."

Tom Kwan, one of their forensic guys, smirked. "I could go all out with the black humor of that comment, but you already look like you're in a black humor so I'll keep my mouth shut."

"Good idea, Kwan." Sean placed the box on one of the chrome tables. He could exchange gallows humor with the best of them. It blew off steam, made the unbearable bearable. But with Elise out there in danger, it didn't seem right.

"When are we getting the finger, and I don't mean from

the captain." Jacoby had burst through another door and stopped short when he saw Sean. "I guess you heard."

"Heard," Sean flicked the box, "and saw. We've got one twisted individual on our hands. I thought he'd kept the finger as a trophy."

"I'm gonna take the print, but we all know it belongs to Katie. Same blue polish, same missing digit. Elise Duran was one lucky lady."

Kwan tapped his chin. "I wonder if he took the finger before or after he killed her. That's gotta hurt."

"I'll leave you to figure that out. I'm outta here." Sean backed out of the lab with a queasy stomach. Kwan's morbid fascinations had never bothered him before. Before Elise.

That's why you never make it personal, son.

His father's voice rumbled up from Sean's subconscious. Where had that come from? Was it something his father actually said to him?

Jacoby's head popped out of the lab door. "Brody, I meant to tell you, I didn't get any prints from Elise's house other than Elise's."

"Yeah, I guess that's what we figured anyway."

"Her house was clean. Doesn't look like she has anyone over—ever."

Sean raised an eyebrow. "And your point?"

Jacoby shrugged his pumped-up shoulders. "Just thought I'd let you know. In case you want to make a move."

"Why, do you?"

"You're the hotshot detective." Jacoby dove back into the lab to dodge the barb Sean was getting ready to fling at him.

Sean dropped into his chair and shuffled through a few messages at his desk. Nothing from Elise. That didn't mean he couldn't check on her. He should've never kissed her, but it didn't mean he couldn't call her. Did it?

He dug into the pocket of his jacket and pulled out Courtney Chu's business card. She'd scribbled her home phone number on the back.

He ran his thumb along the edge of the card once, twice and then punched in the number. With each successive ring, the knots got tighter in his gut. When he got Courtney's voice mail, the words rasped from his dry throat.

"This is Detective Brody. I'm calling..."

"Hello, Sean? It's Elise."

Her breathy voice capped his growing dread, and he slumped in his chair. "For a minute there, I thought you two had gone out."

"My leg's feeling okay but not that good, and Courtney stayed in with me and cooked dinner."

"Your leg's bothering you? Do you need to go back to the hospital?"

"It's throbbing a bit, but I can handle it with a little ibuprofen."

"Take a lot if you need it."

"Any new developments in the case?"

"Some things I can't share."

"Not even with someone who's intimately involved... with the case?"

Sean hunched over his desk and cupped his hand around the receiver. "I'm sorry about...about what happened in the hallway."

"No apology necessary, but an explanation would be nice."

"An explanation?" Maybe he'd have to rethink his appreciation of her forthrightness. "Don't people do that in Montana?"

"Kiss? Yep, lots of that going on in Montana."

"That's a start. I'm glad you recognized the gesture."

"Don't be obtuse, Sean. You kissed me right after you told me to stay out of your life. And I'm not saying people in Montana don't send conflicting messages with their kisses, because they do. I'm saying I don't."

"Can't I just excuse myself by admitting I'm a caveman? I acted on impulse without thinking."

"But you're not the impulsive type, are you?"

"I can be." Especially looking into a pair of big blue eyes.

"If you're so impulsive, tell me what upset you so much tonight."

He cleared his throat. "It was another message from the killer. That's the game he's playing, but I'm glad he's playing it with me now instead of you."

"Whether we like it or not, I'm involved in this and I appreciate your openness."

After Sean hung up the phone, he stared at it until his eyes ached and grew bleary. He hadn't been open with Elise at all, and he had no intention of inviting her into his misery.

THE FOLLOWING MORNING, a dull pain in Elise's leg woke her up and the fear she kept tamping down in her semiconscious state welled to the surface. Closing her eyes, she massaged her thigh around the stitches and took a couple of deep breaths.

Last night she'd sensed Sean holding back, but she couldn't force him to confide in her. She could get through this with or without Sean Brody. With would be better, a lot better.

She stretched her legs and swung them over the side of the bed. Then she shuffled across the hardwood floor and poked her head out the door of Courtney's spare bedroom. Nothing but silence greeted her.

Determined to earn her keep, she shoved her feet into a pair of flip-flops and made her way down to the kitchen.

She blended some plain yogurt with a few berries, sprinkled some granola on top and added a sliced banana.

She found a couple of stale bagels, dropped them into the toaster oven and began pouring water into the coffeemaker.

"Stop right there." A sleepy-eyed Courtney lounged against the entryway to the kitchen, yawning. "The breakfast looks great, but I'll handle the coffee. You don't even drink the stuff."

Elise backed away from the coffeemaker. "It's all yours. I don't want to mess with your morning elixir."

Courtney brushed past her and grabbed a bag of coffee beans. "You did realize you'd have to grind the beans first, didn't you?"

"Of course." Elise dipped a spoon into the yogurt. "How old are the bagels? I figured we could toast away the staleness."

"They're not that old. I have some cream cheese, too." She pointed to the fridge. "How's your leg feeling?"

"Sore. I took some ibuprofen."

"Are you going to stay home from school tomorrow?"

"No way. We have all kinds of activities planned for the last few days of school. It's the best part of the school year."

Courtney pursed her lips as she flipped the switch for the coffee grinder.

When the grating noise stopped, Elise crossed her arms and said, "What? Why are you looking like a disapproving schoolmarm?"

"Maybe you should just take personal leave for the rest of the school year and get out of Dodge."

"You mean turn and run away with my tail between my legs?"

"You're allowed to be a coward. Nobody expects you to hunt this guy down."

Elise curled her fingers into her upper arms. "He had

his second chance to kill me and he sliced my leg instead. He knows I already gave his description to the police, and he's not worried about it because he was wearing a disguise. There's nothing I can do to him now."

"He doesn't know what you told the police. For all he knows, you could remember more details. You're a threat to him, Elise. And that makes him dangerous."

The ringing phone made them both jump. "Who's calling this time of the morning?"

"It's ten o'clock."

Courtney made a face and answered the phone. "Good morning. Yes, she's right here."

She pressed the receiver against her thigh and whispered. "It's the hunky cop."

"Give it over." Elise rolled her eyes and snapped her fingers for the phone. "Hello?"

"Hi, Elise. It's Sean Brody. How are you doing this morning?"

So much better right at this minute.

"I'm good. Leg's a little sore, but that's stitches for you. Any more news since last night?" She hadn't expected to hear his voice last thing before she went to bed and then first thing this morning. Not that she was complaining.

"Nothing new, although the woman at the Presidio may have been a victim of domestic violence. Seems her boyfriend has disappeared." He coughed. "I'm in front of the building on the street. I was just driving by."

"Do you want to come up?"

"I can't leave the car."

"I'll be right down. Give me a minute."

She ended the call and dashed upstairs with Courtney's questions trailing after her. She pulled on her jeans from yesterday and zipped a sweatshirt over her pajama top.

Breathless, she stopped at the front door. "Sean's downstairs. I'm just going to say hello."

"Is this what they call community policing?" Courtney winked.

With her step lighter than it should be, Elise skipped downstairs and squinted as she hit the sidewalk.

Sean waved out the open window of his Crown Vic, and Elise approached the car on the passenger side.

The passenger window slid down, and she hunched over and thrust her head inside the car, resting her arms on the window frame. She inhaled the masculine scent of the car—new leather and fresh soap.

"Thanks for stopping by."

"I was—" he waved his hand vaguely out the window "—in the area. Are you going to get that phone today?"

"I might as well get a permanent phone instead of a pay-as-you-go. I'm not sure I can ever use that other phone again."

"I don't blame you." He opened his car door. "I need to stretch my legs."

He joined her on the sidewalk and wedged his hip against the car. "One of the detectives stopped by the club yesterday and gave them a sketch. Nobody remembers the guy. We're also reviewing some video from some cameras at the bridge and Chinatown. He's going to trip up, Elise."

She scuffed her toe against the cement. "I agree that he's going to screw up, and I appreciate that you're taking the time to keep me informed. Really."

"I know what's it like to be left out of the loop, and while I can't let you in on everything, I don't want to keep you completely in the dark."

His eyes seemed to be looking beyond her face and he'd escaped to that place where she couldn't reach him.

Out of the corner of her eye, she noticed someone moving quickly toward her on the sidewalk. Sean noticed him at the same time. He snapped to attention and his head jerked up as he pushed off the car.

Elise's mouth dropped open and she stumbled back. This was not happening.

Sean caught her as she tripped, and then spun around in a crouch, his fists raised.

She screamed. "Wait! I know him."

"No kidding. I'm Elise's fiancé."

Chapter Nine

Sean lowered his hands, but his fists remained clenched at his sides. He shot a sideways glance at Elise, whose face sported three different shades of red. But she didn't look afraid. Angry, but not afraid.

"What are you doing here, Ty?"

"What do you think? I'm here to take you home."

"I am home." She twisted her head around to look at Courtney's building. "Sort of."

"You don't belong here. You're coming back with me."

Elise made a cross with her fingers and held them in front of her. "No, I'm not. And stop calling yourself my fiancé. That ended a long time ago."

That last line finally made Sean's shoulders relax. He knew Elise wasn't hiding anything.

Not like him.

"Who is this, Elise, and what's he doing here?"

The man threw back his shoulders and his cold blue eyes raked Sean from head to toe. "Who are you?"

"This is ridiculous. Ty, this is Detective Sean Brody. Sean, this is Ty Russell from back home, and I have no idea what he's doing here or how he found me."

Ty took a step back. "I found out what happened to you, and I'm here to bring you back."

Elise closed her eyes and pressed her fingers to her

temples. "How in the world did you find out and how did you find me here?"

"I have my sources."

Elise raked her hands through her loose hair. "Oh, please. Did you con Courtney somehow? Because we both know what a con artist you are."

The man physically flinched as if Elise had slapped him. Obviously, these two had history but it sure didn't sound as if they were engaged anymore—if they ever were.

"Someone attacked you and broke into your house. You're not safe here." He turned to Sean. "Detective, don't you agree?"

He did agree, but he didn't want Elise going back to Montana with this cowboy—her ex-fiancé. And what did he do to become Elise's ex? Must've been something really stupid.

"I'm…we're doing what we can to keep Elise safe. The choice is hers."

Ty narrowed his eyes as his gaze shifted between him and Elise.

Had his feelings for Elise seeped into his voice? What *were* his feelings for Elise?

"Thank you very much." She stamped her bare foot on the ground. "Go home, Ty—alone. I'm not going with you, now or ever."

Ty's face reddened and his face puffed up as if he was about to explode. Had he been abusive toward Elise?

"Step off." Sean inserted himself between Ty and Elise.

Ty sputtered. "Are you kidding me? Why don't you go get yourself a doughnut and leave me to talk some sense into my fiancée?"

"Thanks, but I don't eat doughnuts." Sean drew his shoulders back. "And Elise already told you she's not engaged to you, so giddyap on back to Wyoming."

Ty's mouth gaped open and he bunched his hands in front of him. "It's Montana."

"Whatever." He dropped his gaze to Ty's white-knuckled fists. "Or I can take you in for disturbing the peace."

Ty jabbed his finger in the air. "I'm not giving up on you, Elise. I'll be here for a few days if you change your mind, and if you don't I'll bring your brothers down here with me to this freak-show city to get you home."

"Buh-bye." Elise curled her fingers into a wave. "Try the sourdough bread bowl with clam chowder on your way out of the freak show."

Ty grunted and stalked off, calling over his shoulder, "I'm staying at some dump in Fisherman's Wharf."

"Good. You can get the bread bowl there." She tossed back her hair and sighed. "I can't believe Courtney called him. It had to be her. I thought she was on my side."

"Maybe she was just worried about you and thought it best that you take a break."

She jerked her thumb at Ty's retreating form. "With that?"

"So, what's the story, if you don't mind my asking?"

She dropped onto the low stone wall in front of Courtney's building. "We *were* engaged. We were high school sweethearts and all that stuff, blah, blah, blah."

"He obviously had the stamp of approval from your brothers since he's considering calling them in as reinforcements."

"Oh, yeah, my parents, too."

"And then you grew up? Changed?" He rested his foot on the wall next to her.

"I wish I could claim that, but I was a coward. All the forces in our world were pushing us together and the flow carried me along in its current even though I had misgivings."

"What finally happened to get you to swim against the tide?"

She pinned her hands between her knees and lifted her shoulders. "He cheated on me."

"What an idiot." What man in his right mind would risk losing this woman? "How'd you find out?"

"My maid of honor told me." She raised her eyes to his. "On my wedding day."

"Ouch."

"I didn't want to believe it, at first, but I guess deep down I knew."

"You called off the wedding."

A grin spread across her face. "Not at first."

"What does that mean? You married him and had it annulled?"

"My maid of honor told me while she was helping me dress for the wedding, while all the guests were arriving or sitting in their seats." She stuck her legs in front of her and tapped her toes together like a naughty schoolgirl. "I figured they got all dressed up for the occasion, I might as well give them a show."

"You called it off during the ceremony?" The corner of his mouth twitched into a smile.

"I did. It was a big story in town, even made the local newspaper—runaway bride."

He threw his head back and laughed. No wonder Ty was so desperate to get her back. He had some face to save.

"I walked down the aisle, smiling into the lying face that waited for me under the trellis, and when I got there I exposed him as a liar and a cheat." She pointed her toes. "Then I kicked off my white satin shoes and ran back up the aisle—alone."

"I've never met anyone who ran out on their wedding. That's impressive."

"It was just like a country music video."

"What did old Ty do after that?"

"Came after me, of course, but I wasn't having any of it. My bags were already packed for the honeymoon that never happened, so I threw them in my car and drove to San Francisco."

"And you've been here ever since?"

"I went home once to get the rest of my stuff."

"That's quite a story." He wiped his eyes. "Why this city?"

"The bridge."

His head shot up. "The Golden Gate Bridge?"

"Is there any other?" She linked her fingers and stretched her arms over her head. "My parents took my brothers and me here on a vacation one year. I was fascinated by that bridge, and when we walked across it and I looked back toward the city and out to Alcatraz, I decided then and there I'd come back."

"And here you are."

"The other night when I was out in the bay scrabbling for my life, I almost felt like the bridge was protecting me, looking over me." She glanced up, a blush flagging her cheeks. "Silly, huh?"

"No."

"Anyway—" she stood up and brushed off the seat of her jeans "—that's my sordid story."

"I knew it took guts to escape from a killer, but it really took guts to run out on your wedding."

Screwing up her face, she shook her head. "Not really. I was a wimp. I didn't want to marry Ty even before I found out he'd cheated. I let myself be railroaded by him, my family and what everyone expected of me."

Sean wedged a knuckle beneath her chin. "You're too hard on yourself."

"I just don't think it's all that admirable to run out on a wedding that should've never taken place to begin with."

The radio crackled from the car, and Sean dropped his hand and stuffed it in his pocket before he could do anything stupid again. “Keep safe and get that phone. I’m off tomorrow, but you have my personal cell. Give me a call when you get your new number.”

“Yes, sir.” She saluted. “I’ll probably get it today if the phone store is open.”

He waved and ducked into his car.

Sean kept an eye on Elise in his rearview mirror as she watched his car pull away. She looked small and defenseless against the dark force hanging over her head, but he knew better.

She had a lot of courage and pluck packed into that lithe frame, and she wasn’t the kind of woman to back down from a challenge…or a killer.

THE NEXT MORNING, Elise drove across the Bay Bridge to her school in Oakland. If Ty could see the school where she taught her kindergarteners, he’d kidnap her to take her back to Montana.

She’d confronted Courtney and discovered it was her brother, Oscar, who had called Ty. Once he’d discovered where she lived, Ty had made it a point to contact Oscar, befriend him and enlist him as a spy.

She’d have to give Oscar a piece of her mind when he returned from his trip.

Turning onto the school’s street, she swerved around a trash can that had tumbled from the sidewalk. She slowed down to glare at a couple of older boys hanging out on the street corner. Her kids had to dodge so much just to get to school.

She pulled into the parking lot, dragged her bag from the back and hitched it over her shoulder.

One of the second-grade teachers held the door open for her. “How was your weekend?”

"Not long enough." Elise slipped past the other teacher and headed down the hallway to her classroom. She had no intention of telling anyone at her school about her terrifying brush with a serial killer.

The students hadn't filtered in yet. They lined up outside until the bell rang, and the teachers in the lower grades always escorted their pupils into the school.

Elise unlocked the door to her classroom and bumped it open with her hip. She breathed in the smell of crayons, books and stale bread—all hallmarks of a kindergarten classroom.

"Ready for the last week of school?" Lydia Cummings, one of the other kindergarten teachers, poked her head in the room.

"I don't know." Elise's gaze scanned the colorful artwork tacked up on the walls and the fledgling lima bean plants growing in the windows, finally resting on the big, red number four she'd written on the whiteboard to indicate the number of days left in the school year. "I always miss them over the summer until I get the new batch in the fall."

"Spoken like a true kindergarten teacher." Lydia gave her a misty smile. "We're really lucky you came to us this year."

"I feel exactly the same way." Elise pulled a new book and a deflated beach ball out of her bag and dropped them on her desk before leaving to collect her students.

She tugged her sweater around her body and held it closed with folded arms as she walked onto the playground shrouded in a gray mist indistinguishable from the blacktop. Kids scurried between the white lines to get in place before the bell rang.

She approached the line for her classroom, which resembled a worm, wriggling this way and that.

Three of her students chanted in unison, "Good morning, Miss Duran."

"Good morning." She put on her brightest smile.

A small boy darted from the line and wrapped his arms around her legs in a kindergarten hug.

She patted his back. "Good morning, Eli."

This is what she'd miss over the summer, this pure, honest affection—no deceit, no subterfuge.

The bell blared over the playground, and the older kids shuffled off to their classes, bumping each other and snickering at private jokes. Elise clapped her hands. "Here we go."

The line of squiggling children wended its way through the double doors down the hallway to the kindergarten rooms.

The kids sensed their impending freedom in four days. Restlessness bubbled throughout the classroom, and Elise had to raise her voice and rap on her desktop more than once to get her students back on task.

Her gaze wandered to the big clock on the wall several times. The antsy kids were having an effect on her. Finally the bell rang for recess and lunch. Elise escorted her kids to the playground and then headed for the teachers' lounge to grab some lunch. The kinder teachers rotated lunchtime duty every day, two of them helping the aides and two enjoying the luxury of lunch in the staff room.

Elise popped the lid of a plastic container of Courtney's leftover pasta and shoved it into the microwave. She turned toward Viola, the other teacher on break. "Are you headed to Alabama right after school ends or later in the summer?"

"Leaving next week." Viola kicked off her shoes and propped her feet up on the chair across from her. "I'm enjoying the cool weather while I can, although I'm kind of looking forward to getting out of the city."

"Really?" The microwave beeped and Elise removed her container and carried it to the table next to Viola's.

"You were dreading the thought of heat and humidity and extended family just a few weeks ago."

Viola wiggled her toes and glanced up from her smartphone. "That's before we had a killer on the loose."

Elise's hand jerked and the steam burned her wrist. She dropped the lid. "Y-you mean that woman found by the bay?"

"She's not the only one."

"She's not?" Elise's throat tightened. Had there been another murder? Sean hadn't mentioned anything on the phone last night when she'd called him with her new number. Had they finally tied the woman at the Presidio to this killer?

Viola shook her head. "Not yet, but there was another one that got away."

"When was that?" Viola must be referring to her attack. The SFPD had been trying to keep Elise's encounter out of the press, just as they were trying to keep particular aspects of Katie's murder a secret, despite that reporter's best efforts. They had to do that. Sean had to keep certain secrets.

"Not sure. Friday night. No details on that one, but the police suspect it was the same guy who murdered the other one." Viola hunched her shoulders and dropped her phone. "I hate it when stuff like this happens."

"Me, too."

The phone on the lunchroom wall rang, and they both jumped. Elise shoved back from the table and grabbed the receiver. "Lunchroom."

"Elise, is that you?"

"Yep."

"I got a call in the front office for you. He's still on the line, so I'm going to transfer him over."

Elise swallowed. "Okay."

"Go ahead, sir."

"Did you change your phone number because of me?"

She heaved out a sigh and rolled her eyes at Viola. "No, Ty. I had to get a new phone and a new number. Why don't you just go home?"

"I've been doing a little investigating of that Detective Brody. You're not going to like…"

"What I don't like is you harassing me. For the millionth time, I'm not going home with you—now or ever. Give it up and move on. It's been over a year. Don't call me again." She slammed the receiver home.

"Girl, is that the ex-fiancé?"

"He came all the way here to take me home. What's he going to do, kidnap me?"

She shook her head. "Men. They don't want you unless they can't have you."

They finished lunch discussing more pleasant topics, such as the end-of-the-school-year party. Elise hadn't felt like telling Viola that Ty had come here to rescue her from a killer. That she was the one who got away. She didn't want to be the object of anyone's pity or amazement or projected fear.

The door to the teachers' lounge burst open and Mrs. McKinney, the senior kindergarten teacher, charged through clutching Eli's arm.

Eli turned his round eyes on Elise, his mouth a matching circle.

Elise jumped up. She didn't like Mrs. McKinney's disciplinary methods with the kids, and Eli looked scared out of his wits. "What's going on?"

"This young man was disobeying school rules on the playground."

"But he told me. He gave me…"

"Silence, young man."

Elise crossed the room and took Eli's hand, pulling him

away from Mrs. McKinney's clutches. "What happened, Eli?"

Mrs. McKinney butted in. "I spotted Eli on the far side of the playground on the grass by the gate. He's not supposed to be outside of the kindergarten play area."

Elise squeezed Eli's hand. "You need to stay on our playground, Eli. Miss Ellen and Mrs. Dory can't watch you way over there."

"That's not all, Miss Duran." Mrs. McKinney thrust out her formidable bosom. "Eli was talking to a stranger at the fence."

Elise tapped Eli's brown cheek with her finger. "You're not supposed to talk to strangers, Eli. Promise Mrs. McKinney you won't do that again."

Eli dropped his gaze and scuffed the toe of his Converse sneakers against the linoleum floor, shoving his hand in the front pocket of his jeans. "I promise."

She smiled. "That's better. Are you satisfied, Mrs. McKinney? I don't think Eli needs to go to Principal Yarborough."

Mrs. McKinney huffed. "I suppose not, but we can't have these kids wandering around the playground and talking to strangers."

"Okay. That's settled, then. You can walk to the line with me, Eli." She held out her hand and wiggled her fingers.

He buried his hand deeper in his pocket and jutted out his lower lip. "But he gave me something."

"Candy?" Mrs. McKinney snapped her head around. "Did he give you candy, Eli? Hand it over."

"N-no." His big brown eyes met Elise's. "He gave me something for you, Miss Duran."

Elise's stomach dropped and she grabbed on to the back of the chair. "What do you mean, Eli? The stranger you were talking to at the gate gave you something to give to me?"

"Yes." He bobbed his head up and down.

Viola cleared her throat and whispered, "Maybe it was your crazy ex."

Maybe it was Sean. "Was he a police officer?"

"Yes, Miss Duran." He slid a sideways glance at Mrs. McKinney that tried to put her in her place.

Elise's pulse quickened. It must've been Sean checking up on her, but he should've just come into her classroom. He should know better than to bother the children.

"What did he give you?" Mrs. McKinney's eyes narrowed.

Eli dragged his hand out of his pocket, a crumpled piece of white paper in his fist. "Here. He gave me this."

Viola raised her brows and shook her finger at Elise. "Why is a cop coming to school and sending you notes?"

Elise's cheeks warmed as she flipped open the folded piece of paper. The words swam before her eyes, and the blood in her veins turned to ice water.

"What does it say, Elise?" Viola took a step forward.

Elise raised her eyes from the note and blinked, bringing Viola's face, lined with worry, into focus. Then she glanced down at Eli, his usually sweet face contorted by fear.

She dropped to her knees in front of him and tweaked his nose. "Thank you for bringing the note to me, Eli. But promise me you'll never talk to a stranger like that again."

"I promise, Miss Duran." His lower lip trembled. "I-is the note bad?"

"This?" She waved it in the air. "Not at all. Mrs. McKinney's going to take you back outside to play, but stay in the kinder yard."

A tremulous smile wobbled across his face. "Yes, Miss Duran."

Mrs. McKinney shot her a worried look. "Let's go, young man. I heard you're the only kindergartner who can hop on one foot all the way across the blacktop, and I want to see that before the bell rings."

Elise mouthed *thank you* over Eli's head and transferred his grimy little hand from hers to Mrs. McKinney's.

When the door closed behind them, Viola spun around. "What is in that note?"

Elise took a deep breath and read aloud. "'One plus one equal 187. Six plus twelve equal 187. Thirty-seven plus forty-nine plus 122 plus twenty-eight equal 187. 187 for you.'"

Viola cocked her head and plucked the note from Elise's fingers.

Elise rubbed her damp hands against her skirt and swallowed. "I have no idea what it means, but it's probably related to something that happened this past weekend."

"Elise, you know my husband's a cop with the Oakland P.D."

"Yeah, I know that, but I'm sort of already working with the SFPD on this."

Viola shook her head. "It's not that, but I know what 187 means in cop-speak, anyway."

"What does it mean?"

"Murder."

Chapter Ten

"Why is he doing this?" Elise sat on a table strewn with colorful wooden blocks, one leg crossed over the other, kicking back and forth.

"For fun. For attention. He's a sick SOB. The rules don't apply to him."

Sean paced in front of her. The Oakland P.D. had already been out to question the boy and get a description, which had been useless—a white man with a baseball cap and sunglasses is all Eli could give them. Oh, yeah, and the stranger had a badge.

That last bit of information had punched him in the gut—not as if any Tom, Dick or Harry couldn't get a fake badge to fool a kid.

The teachers on playground duty hadn't been much more helpful than Eli. Mrs. McKinney had seen him from a distance. The stranger must've seen her barreling toward him because before she'd made it halfway across the field, he'd hightailed it out of there. He'd completed his business anyway. He'd given Eli the note to give to Elise.

Why was he harassing Elise? It wasn't good enough for him to taunt the lead detective on the case?

"How did he know where I taught? Do you think the kids are safe?"

Sean stopped pacing and flicked the leaf of a plant

growing in the well of an egg carton. “He had your purse, your wallet, your phone. He probably figured out the name of your school from something in your purse.”

“My paycheck stub.” She hit her forehead with the heel of her hand. “I had picked it up from the mailbox that night and crammed it into my bag.”

“That made it easy for him.”

“And the kids?” She hopped from the table and took up the pacing where he’d left off. “Do you think he’ll do anything to the kids? I couldn’t stand it if something happened to any one of them.”

She covered her face with her hands and choked out a sob.

Despite his better judgment, he readied himself to go to her, to comfort her, but she looked up at him with dry eyes and a tight mouth.

“If he so much as touches one of these kids, I’ll take care of him myself. I still have my .22 at home.”

Her ferocity called to him even more than her pain. On his way to her side, he tripped over one of the little plastic chairs, which tipped over and bounced once before he caught it.

He righted it and then put an arm around Elise’s rigid shoulders. “He’s not interested in those kids, but the Oakland P.D. is going to have a patrol car here during school hours for the rest of the week. Doesn’t hurt that one of the officer’s wives works here.”

“Viola Crouch. She teaches kinder with me. She’s the one who told me what ‘187’ meant.” She shivered beneath his arm. “If he knows that and has a badge, maybe he’s a cop.”

Sean dropped his arm and turned away. “A lot of people know that 187 is the penal code for homicide, especially if they follow crimes, and anyone can pick up a fake badge.”

“I’m sorry.” She touched his back. “I didn’t mean to

insult you or your profession, but it does happen, doesn't it? I read somewhere that a few arsonists actually become firefighters or arson investigators."

"It happens." What was happening to his cool, calm demeanor? He'd always prided himself on his poker face, and now he was allowing all kinds of emotions to spill over for this woman to read. Or could she just see through his barriers easily?

"I suppose there won't be any fingerprints on the note or the gate since Eli said the man was wearing gloves, not to mention Eli handled the note and Viola and I touched it, as well."

"He's arrogant, but he's not stupid. He's not going to get caught over a set of fingerprints. The Oakland cops looked anyway and they'll let us know."

"What do you think those numbers mean, other than the 187?"

"I don't know, but we'll find out. These guys aren't as clever as they think they are." Sean traced his fingers along the edges of the blocks. "It's getting late. Why don't you get out of here?"

"Three more days." She strolled to the whiteboard and erased the number four, grabbed a red marker and wrote *three* in its place. Then she changed the date in the upper-right corner of the board for tomorrow.

Sean focused on the date and approached the whiteboard, his muscles tense. "It's June twelfth tomorrow."

"Our last day is the…" She dropped the marker and spun around. "It's six, twelve tomorrow."

"One plus one equals 187, and six plus twelve equals 187."

"He's going to kill again tomorrow. One plus one?"

"Maybe he's going to kill more than one person."

Elise put her hands over her eyes as if she could block

out the truth. "Why is he telling me? I don't want to know this."

This time he did take her in his arms—hard. He pulled her against his chest and wrapped his arms around her body. She stiffened for a second. He knew she wanted to stand on her own, but then she melted against him, her arms curling around his waist.

The trembling of her body subsided, and Sean stroked her silky hair.

Sighing, she tipped back her head. "I guess I am involved in your work, whether you like it or not. He's sending messages to both of us now."

"I definitely don't like it, but this does have a weird silver lining."

Her eyes widened, and he felt her heart pick up speed.

Did she think he was going to admit having her in his arms was the silver lining? Not even that could make it okay that she'd become the obsession of some serial killer.

"Since he's communicating with you, he's not going to want to hurt you. For whatever reason, he wants to brag to you, keep you in his sick loop. For now, that's keeping you safe."

She dropped her head in a sharp nod and pulled away from him. "I guess that's something."

He'd disappointed her, and he immediately wanted to make it up to her. "I'm going to follow you back to your friend's place."

"That's not necessary." She hoisted her school bag over one shoulder and her purse over the other. "Didn't you just say I was safe as long as he was still communicating with me?"

"*Safe* is a relative term. What are your plans for dinner?" He flicked off the lights of her classroom and stepped into the hallway as she pulled the door shut and locked it.

"Food." She spun away from her classroom door, and

her low heels clicked on the floor as Sean tried to keep up with her.

She unlocked her car door and he stepped in front of her to open it for her. "Is Courtney going to be home?"

"I'm not sure." She opened the back door of her car and tossed her bag inside. "She sometimes sees clients late so they can come in after work."

That's all he needed to hear. He didn't want to leave her on her own. "I'll be right on your tail just to make sure you get back to her place safely."

Elise wheeled out of the parking lot and Sean followed her through the rough neighborhood. It didn't surprise him that she taught the kids in this area, and they needed a teacher like Elise—strong and fearless and willing to go up against a killer for them.

He tailed her across the Bay Bridge, and that other bridge invaded his thoughts. Why had this killer chosen to dump his victim in view of the Golden Gate? Was it a nod to those other murders so many years ago? The murders that impacted his life, formed him, shaped him?

He rubbed his knuckles across his tattoo—a Phoenix that symbolized his rise from the ashes of his early life. A life that threatened to stake its claim over him with these recent murders.

Twenty minutes later, he turned onto Courtney's street and watched Elise's taillights disappear into the underground parking garage. He pulled to the curb and exited his vehicle. He waited by the building's entrance until Elise peeked out the window, cupping her hand around her face. The electronic lock clicked and he pulled open the door.

"That's not a bad commute for you to your own place, either."

"It's a lot better when I leave school at my regular time. You know, the days I'm not involved in a police investigation."

He jerked his thumb toward the garage. “Is Courtney home yet?”

“No.”

“Do you want to share some dinner with me?”

“Dinner?” She folded her arms across her chest and gripped the straps of her bags.

“My stomach was growling all the way over, so I ordered some Italian to be delivered here.” He spread his hands. “It would be a lot better if I could eat my dinner here and share it with you instead of hauling it home to eat by myself.”

She hunched her shoulders. “Is that allowed? Are you still working?”

“I thought I told you. I have the day off today. Can’t you tell?” He plucked at his T-shirt. “I think I’m allowed to eat where I want on my day off.”

A small red car squealed to a stop at the curb.

“I think that’s your dinner now.” She pointed out the door as the driver climbed out of his car and popped his trunk.

“*Our* dinner. A little ravioli, eggplant parmigiana, chopped salad, garlic bread.”

“Is there enough for two?”

“I ordered for two. Even if I didn’t, you don’t look like you could make much of a dent in a pile of ravioli.”

She snorted. “You’d be surprised.” She stepped around him and pushed the door wide, gesturing to the driver. “Get that food up here.”

The kid stumbled, his eyes darting from Sean to Elise.

Sean laughed. “It’s okay. She’s harmless, just hungry.”

The delivery boy thrust the box, piled with white paper bags, toward Sean.

Sean dug into his pocket for some bills and paid the kid. “Lead the way.”

By the time they got to Courtney's door, the smell of garlic filled the hallway.

Elise stepped into the condo and pulled him in after her. "Quick, before Courtney's neighbors riot. They're a snooty bunch."

He placed the bags on the granite countertop of the kitchen's center island. "Restroom?"

She pointed to a door across from the staircase.

By the time he returned, she'd pulled plates, bowls and silverware from the cupboards and drawers.

He lifted the foil tins from the bags and removed their covers. Steam rose from the dishes, and Sean's mouth watered.

Elise scooped up the salad and dropped it into the two bowls with her head tilted to one side. "You actually laughed down there."

He tore a piece of garlic bread from the loaf and bit into it, a warm trickle of butter running down his chin. He blotted his face with a napkin while he chewed. "I do occasionally laugh. I am human."

And despite the circumstances, he felt more human than he had in a long time. Despite the death all around him, more alive.

"Well, I like it." She popped the lid off a plastic container full of salad dressing and held it above one of the salad bowls. "Do you want me to do the honors, or do you prefer to put your own dressing on?"

"Dump it on there." He pulled another piece of bread from the loaf and held it to her lips. "You gotta try this."

She ducked her head and sank her teeth into the spongy part of the bread, soaked with garlic butter, which dribbled out of the corner of her mouth. Raising her eyes to the ceiling, she murmured, "Mmm."

"You have—" he dabbed the corner of a napkin on her luscious lips "—a little bit of butter right there."

"Charming. That's almost as bad as having spinach between your teeth."

"Blame it on the bread." He picked up the salad bowls and walked to a round table next to the sliding glass doors that led to a balcony that overlooked the city.

Elise followed him with the pasta and bread. "Do you want something to drink? I'm sure Courtney has some wine around here."

"Just water."

"Oh, are you not allowed to drink even a little when you're driving?"

He reached for the silverware and arranged it on the two placemats. "As long as I'm not working it's okay, just like anyone if I stay under the legal limit. But I usually never drink and drive. I'm fine with water. Don't let me stop you."

"I told you the other night I'm not much of a drinker." She wrinkled her nose. "It's a good thing, too, because I may not have regained consciousness so fast in that trunk."

It always came back to that. The laughter, the food, the sexual tension between them—none of it mattered, none of it would've been possible if some maniac hadn't stuffed Elise in the trunk of his car.

But Sean would do his best to make it normal, and for the remainder of the meal he tried to do just that.

He held up a spoon full of pasta. "More ravioli?"

Elise pushed her chair away from the table and patted her flat tummy. "I'm stuffed. I had pasta for dinner last night and for lunch today, too. With all that carb loading, I could probably run a marathon tomorrow."

"Sorry, I could've ordered Chinese."

"Had it for lunch yesterday."

"Greek?" He lifted one eyebrow.

"I don't think I've ever had Greek food." She dabbed

at a crumb of bread with her fingertip and sucked it into her mouth.

"We'll have to remedy that sometime. There's a great little place in North Beach, right smack in the middle of all the Italian places." The words came out automatically as if this were a regular date with a regular woman.

There was nothing regular about this date—or Elise Duran.

She stood up abruptly and grabbed the rim of her plate with both hands. "Are you still eating, or can I take your plate?"

He handed her the plate. "You can take it, but I'll do the cleanup since I sort of invited myself over."

"We'll both do it. I'll wrap up the food. If you can rinse the dishes, I'll stick them in the dishwasher."

"Deal." He gathered the silverware and glasses and followed her to the kitchen. He ran the warm water and swiped a dish sponge across the streaks of tomato sauce and bits of cheese stuck to the plates.

Elise replaced the lids on the food containers and glanced over her shoulder. "You're pretty good at that for a single guy, or maybe that's why you *are* so good at it since you have to fend for yourself in the kitchen."

"Believe me, I got a lot of practice growing up."

"Ah, was your mom one of those liberated women who believed in teaching her sons how to do housework? Sounds like my kinda woman."

He ducked his head to scrub at a stubborn piece of cheese. "My mom was…ill. My brothers and I did most of the work around the house."

"Oh, I'm sorry. That must've been tough on your dad, too."

Why the hell had he brought up his childhood? A voice in the back of his head chided. *You're the one who wanted this to be a regular date.*

"My dad..."

"Who opened an Italian eatery in my place and forgot to tell me?"

Courtney burst through the front door to save the day. She waved a hand in front of her nose. "I can smell that garlic all the way down the hallway. The homeowners' association is going to bring it up in their next meeting and give me a lecture."

She dropped a laptop case and a leather briefcase in the corner of the room and spun around. "Oh, hello."

Sean lifted a soapy hand. "Hope you don't mind me barging in."

Courtney's dark eyes darted from his face to Elise's. "Nope. How was your day, Elise? Those little monsters still running you ragged?"

"My kids are not little monsters. How about you? Busy day?"

"I saw a new client today. Those first sessions are always a little rough." Courtney checked her phone and then connected it to her charger on the counter.

"Do you want some food before I finish wrapping it up?" Elise held up one of the containers.

"That's okay." Courtney pointed to her bags. "I picked up a sandwich in my building before I left, but I will have a glass of wine while you tell me what happened today that a cop has to follow you home and eat dinner with you."

Elise sighed and stood on her tiptoes to reach for a bottle of wine in the cupboard. "If you insist."

She opened the bottle and splashed a quantity of the ruby liquid in the glass. When she carried it to her friend, Sean joined them at the table.

Courtney sipped her wine as Elise told her what had happened at her school.

When she finished, Courtney threw back the rest of

her wine and held out her glass for a refill. "That's creepy, Elise. How did he know where you taught?"

Elise reached behind her for the bottle. "I had a pay stub in my purse. He probably got it from there. He may have even seen something on my phone. Heck, maybe he even did a search for me on the internet. It's not like he doesn't already know my name and address."

Courtney turned to Sean. "What do those numbers mean?"

He slumped in the chair and stretched his legs in front of him. "The penal code for murder is 187. We figured the one plus one means two murders or two people. The six and twelve might mean tomorrow's date."

Courtney had covered her mouth with her hand, and it slid to her throat. "What about the other numbers?"

"Don't know yet. I sent the note to the station, and one of the detectives is working on deciphering it."

"Do you think there's going to be another murder tomorrow?"

"If so, I hope the other numbers tell us where."

"Who, what, when, where and how." Elise took a sip of Courtney's wine and puckered her lips. "Is that obnoxious journalist still bothering you?"

"What are you implying? Do you think he's involved somehow?"

"Seems awfully anxious to get some big scoop."

"That's his job. It doesn't mean he's a killer."

Courtney snapped her fingers. "I know that guy. Ray Lopez, right? I've seen him on the local news. He's a big mouth, but he's entertaining in a tabloid kinda way."

"Yeah, that's him. You've seen him do other stories?" Elise asked.

"He has that half-hour show after the news. I heard his promo today, and he's going to feature Katie Duncan's murder."

"Great." Sean rolled his eyes. He just hoped none of the officers had talked to Lopez and revealed any of the details they wanted to keep hidden from the public—like the severed finger.

"In fact—" Courtney rose from the table and stepped down into the living room, where she swept the remote from the coffee table "—I think he's on right now."

A commercial blared from the TV and Courtney tossed the remote on the couch. "I'm going to soak in the tub and scrub off my clients' troubles. I'm sure I'll see you later, Detective Brody."

"Sean, and sorry again for intruding on your space."

She waved a manicured hand. "Any…friend of Elise's is welcome as long as she's staying here."

Sean turned back to the TV just as Lopez's program began. As Courtney promised, Lopez jumped right into Katie Duncan's murder and connected it to Elise's escape the night before, although he didn't mention Elise's name on the air.

Lopez stared into the camera. "The autopsy report on Katie isn't finished yet, but preliminary reports suggest she received a blow to the head before she was sliced."

"You didn't tell me that." Elise crossed her arms and perched on the arm of the couch.

"Didn't think I had to. We knew her murder was connected to your assailant."

The next shot featured Lopez stationed in front of the Speakeasy, and Elise's grip on her upper arms tightened.

"In the attack in front of this club, the killer pretended to be injured with a cast on his arm, and then used the plaster cast to viciously hit the victim over the head. This incapacitated her, and he was able to stuff her into the trunk of his vehicle."

Lopez went on to describe the vehicle and show Elise's composite sketch.

"We can turn this off." Sean reached for the remote, but Elise snatched it up first.

"Wait. I want to watch the rest."

As the half-hour show drew to a close, Lopez was back in the studio. "The interesting thing about these murders is that this city has seen something like this before."

Sean's eye twitched and he tightened his jaw. He wanted to punch his fist through the TV as Lopez continued blabbing.

"Almost twenty years ago, another serial killer in the city used the same M.O. He feigned an injury to lure in his victims, knocked them out and then cut them to ribbons."

Elise murmured something that Sean couldn't hear over the pounding in his head.

"That serial killer murdered five women but was never caught. And the strangest thing about that old case and this new one?" He paused for dramatic effect. "The killer twenty years ago was communicating with SFPD Homicide Detective Joseph Brody, and the current killer is communicating with Brody's son, SFPD Homicide Detective Sean Brody."

Elise gasped. "Sean?"

And then there it was. A picture of a young officer with dark hair and brooding eyes.

Not satisfied, Lopez continued in his awed voice. "The story gets even more bizarre. Detective Joseph Brody was actually suspected of being the murderer, and the killings stopped after Brody threw himself from the Golden Gate Bridge."

Chapter Eleven

The remote fell from Elise's hands, and she flinched as it hit the table. "Sean?"

Without turning to face her, he leaned sideways and grabbed the remote control, the muscles in his forearm corded and tense.

The TV went silent although Ray Lopez was still moving his lips.

"I-is all that true, what he said about your father?" She licked her lips, and her gaze dropped to his tattoo. What else had he been keeping from her?

He placed the remote on the coffee table with a click, put his hands on his knees and pushed up from the couch. He took one turn around the room and then stopped in front of her.

"It's not true." He dragged a hand through his hair. "It is true."

She searched his face, the muscle ticking in his jaw, the deep grooves on each side of his mouth. "Just tell me the truth, Sean. I want to know the truth."

"My father was a homicide detective, and there was a string of murders—similar to Katie Duncan's but not exactly."

"Like Lopez said, the M.O. was the same? The killer used some fake infirmity to trick his victims?"

"Yes." He ran the back of his hand across his mouth. "Faked an injury to catch the victims off guard."

"The killer communicated with your father?"

"He did, but I told you before, that's not so uncommon."

She folded her hands in front of her, twisting her fingers. "What about the other part? Was your father really suspected of being the killer?"

Sean slammed his fist into his palm. "That's a lie. My father never killed anyone."

"Except himself."

Sean's face blanched, and his lips tightened. "At the height of the investigation, someone witnessed a man jumping from the bridge and items belonging to my father were found there. The Coast Guard never found his body."

"I'm sorry." The words bubbled to her lips. How could she be angry with him for withholding the truth from her when such pain filled his eyes?

Squeezing those eyes shut, he pinched the bridge of his nose. "Because of his suicide and because the killing stopped afterward, the department suspected him, but nobody was ever able to prove anything—not even that he committed suicide."

"You don't believe he killed himself even though his stuff was left on the bridge?"

"I don't think he would've done that to us. We got nothing. His life insurance wouldn't pay out and neither would the department."

"Sean." She reached out and trailed her fingers down his arm. When they skimmed over his tattoo, she snatched her hand back.

"What about the rest of it? Was there any proof that he was the killer?"

Sean plowed a hand through his hair again. "There was plaster of Paris in his patrol car. But would he really be stupid enough to leave that in his patrol car? Someone planted it."

"You think someone was setting him up for the murders?"

"Absolutely. There's no way…my father could never be capable of anything like that."

Of course he'd say that about his father. He'd been a boy. How could he know for sure?

"Why would someone set him up? Who?"

"You don't think I've gone through this in my mind a million times? I can only guess, but I think it was probably the real killer. He taunted my father and then set him up so he could get away with murder."

"The murders stopped when your father…killed himself?"

"Exactly." Sean smacked a hand on the counter. "That was the whole point. It got the killer off the hook."

"And then he just stopped killing? Isn't it unusual for a serial killer to stop on his own?"

"It's not typical, but it does happen. Besides, how do we know he didn't move to some other big city to continue his spree?"

She held out her hand. "Wait a minute. So you think a serial killer made contact with your dad and when your dad starting closing in, the killer started planting evidence implicating your father? When your father jumped, the killer packed up and started plying his trade somewhere else to escape?"

Sean nodded as he clenched his hands into fists.

"Why would your father commit suicide? Was the evidence against him that strong?"

"I don't know. That's the hardest piece of this puzzle for me to figure out. My dad—he wasn't one to run from a fight. If he was innocent, and I know he was, he would've stood up to his accusers. He would've proved his innocence."

Elise edged through the space between them, vibrating with tension, with a slow, cautious gait. She placed her hand on Sean's tight arm. "But he didn't do that, Sean."

Raw emotion flashed across his face, twisting his features into a mask of pain.

Trailing her fingers across his tense jawline, she whispered, "I'm sorry."

His chest heaved and he caught her hand in his warm grip. "I can't figure out why he did it, Elise. I know he's no killer, but I guess he was a coward."

"You were a child, Sean." She squeezed his hand. "You can't know what demons he faced. You can't get into someone's head like that."

His lips twisted and he raised his eyes to the ceiling. "Courtney thinks she can."

"And maybe if your father had been able to see a good therapist like Courtney, she could've gotten inside his head."

Sean's eyes widened and he brought her hand to his lips and kissed her knuckles. "You've just given me a great idea."

With the impression of his lips still burning her skin, Elise smiled. "Do you want me to get Courtney down here so she can shrink your head?"

"No, thanks." He dropped her hand and took a turn around the room. "I went through my father's files when I started working with the department, and I noticed that he'd been referred to a psychologist specializing in law enforcement issues. The referral had been made when the killer started communicating with him, before he became a suspect in the killings."

"Did he go?"

"I don't know. I didn't follow up on it."

Missing his touch, she crossed her arms and pulled out a chair from the kitchen table. "Courtney would be the first one to tell you about client confidentiality. You can't go barging into a therapist's office asking about his or her patients."

"Even after twenty years? Even if the patient is dead?" He parked himself on the arm of Courtney's white brocade couch.

"I don't know how long confidentiality lasts. What are you hoping to find?"

"Answers, Elise. I need answers, especially because I'm afraid the whole thing is happening again."

"Was the therapist's name in your father's file?"

Sean scratched his chin. "No, but the department uses the same ones, so I'm sure I'll be able to find out whom we were using back then. Plus, I have my sources in the department."

"Would the powers that be allow you to reopen your father's case?"

He snorted. "Not likely. They'd rather forget about it. I'm sure there were plenty in the department who didn't want to hire me in the first place. If I start making trouble, that faction will use that as justification."

"But you still have sources?"

"Yeah. One of the most powerful people in the department."

"Chief Stoddard?"

"Chief Marie." He winked.

"Who's Chief Marie?"

"Marie Giardano. She keeps our records."

"Ah, friends in high places."

"She worked there when my father did, and she knew both of my parents. She never believed he was the Phone Book Killer, either."

She raised her eyebrows at the name. "I'm assuming he picked his victims out of the phone book?"

"In alphabetical order, starting with the letter D."

Gasping, Elise clutched her throat. "Just like Duran and Duncan."

"You see why it looks like déjà vu to me?"

"Sean—" she reached out and traced her fingertips along the wings of his tattoo "—do you think your ink has anything to do with it?"

He shivered beneath her touch. "Of course I thought about it. That's why I freaked out in a totally unprofessional manner when you told me about your attacker's tattoo."

"Do you think he's some kind of copycat?" She covered her mouth with her hands. "Is that what the message on my mirror was all about?" She cinched his arm. "Is someone going to start trying to pin these murders on you?"

"I can't say the thought didn't cross my mind."

"Why didn't you tell me all this before?"

He placed his hands on her shoulders, wedging his thumbs against her collarbones. "I didn't want to drag you into all of this, Elise. It's ancient history to most people, but it haunts me every day, every day I catch a glimpse of the bridge."

Her heart ached for this man and the burden he carried. Her issues with her family and Ty seemed trivial compared with Sean Brody's family legacy.

She encircled his wrists with her fingers. "I am involved, Sean, and it's not ancient history to me. It's my story, right now. And I want to help you in any way I can."

His dark eyes burned into hers, and she didn't look away. She didn't ever want to look away. She wanted to get lost in the depths of his soul and bring light to his darkness.

When his lips touched hers, they scorched her with

their heat and passion. She sagged against his chest, and he wrapped one arm around her waist.

He deepened the kiss and she drank him in, getting drunk on the sensations that swirled through her body. Who needed wine? She had Sean Brody.

Courtney yelped from the top of the stairs, and they jumped apart.

She called down. "This new client is going to be a pain. First session today, and he's already calling me after hours."

Elise rolled her eyes at Sean. "Is it an emergency?"

"He thinks so, but I talked him down from the ledge, so to speak." Courtney stopped on the staircase, clutching her phone in her hand. "Oh, I'm sorry. I didn't realize you were still here, Sean."

He held up his hand. "I'm on my way out."

"Don't let me scare you away." She drew a circle around her face, which was caked with green paste. "When this comes off, I'm more beautiful than ever."

Elise slipped her arm through his. "I'll walk you out. Thanks for dinner."

"My pleasure." He brushed a loose strand of hair from her cheek. "I hope you're feeling better after today's events."

"I feel fine, but it'll be nice having the Oakland P.D. patrolling the school this week."

"And your leg?"

"Stiff and sore, but it could be worse, right?"

"You're tough, kid."

"It's like you said before. He's going to make a mistake soon."

He cupped her face with one hand and brushed his lips against hers. "I just don't want you getting burned."

As she watched him walk down the hallway to the elevator, she murmured, “Too late for that, Sean Brody. Too late for that.”

Chapter Twelve

Sean hunched over the counter, studied Marie's lined face and gave her his best smile. "I know where the boxes are, Marie."

She tapped a pen on top of the log book. "You should. You've practically worn a path in the linoleum back there over the years."

He plucked the pen from her fingers, the long red fingernails at odds with her age-spotted skin, and slid the log book toward him.

Marie snatched it away. "You don't need to sign in, Sean."

He lifted one eyebrow. "Since when?"

"Since the brass has been snooping through the books."

His pulse jumped. "Looking for what?"

"Your guess is as good as mine." She raised her plump shoulders. "I just don't think they need to see your name written in ink checking out your dad's case files again. Especially now."

He leaned in closer, his breath fogging the glass in the window. "What are you hearing?"

"I'm hearing a killer has you on speed dial."

"And?" He licked his lips.

"Just that."

Sean dropped the pen. "Maybe I don't need to look through the boxes again."

"Be my guest. I won't remember that you were here. My memory is notoriously bad on Tuesdays."

"Even Tuesdays twenty years ago?"

"Mmm, back then I had trouble with Saturdays." She put her finger on the side of her prominent nose. "What am I supposed to recall about twenty years in the past besides the fact that I had cleavage that could cause whiplash?"

"You still got it, Marie."

"You Brody boys are all charmers." She tapped on the glass with one of her long nails. "Tell me what you need."

Sean folded his hands on top of the log book, pressing his thumbs together. "Who did the department use for therapy in those days? You know, for officer-involved shootings, alcoholism, the works."

She laughed, a sharp bark that filled the small front office of the records room. "I thought you were going to test me, Brody."

"You remember without even looking?"

"The department used only one guy in those days, and we had him for eighteen years. Dr. James Patrick. He retired just seven years ago. That's who your dad would've seen."

"Did he see him?"

Marie looked both ways. "I don't know, but I do know they made the recommendation. Usually when the department makes the recommendation, you'd better follow through or it could be your job."

"It wound up being his life."

Marie reached through the space under the window and patted Sean's arm. "He must've had a good reason to do that, Sean, leaving you and your brothers and Joanne. Someone or something drove him to it, and I don't believe for one minute it was guilt over any murders."

"I appreciate that, Marie."

She coughed her smoker's cough. "If you appreciate it so much, why don't you send those good-looking brothers of yours over here to visit an old lady?"

"I'll get right on it—after I solve this case."

"Which case, Sean?"

He slapped the log book. "You're a lifesaver, Marie."

He jogged up two flights of stairs and paused at the fire door, pulling out his phone. He typed in a quick text to Elise, and she responded immediately that everything was fine.

Blowing out a long breath, he pulled open the door and crossed the hall to the homicide division. When he got to his desk, he shoved Curtis off the edge. "Go sit on your own desk."

Curtis waved a piece of paper in the air. "You wouldn't say that if you knew what I had in my hand."

"A first-class ticket to paradise? 'Cuz that's what I need about now." *Two* first-class tickets to paradise.

"Almost as good." He slapped the paper on Sean's desk. "Patterson ran the numbers from the note through a few computer programs and came up with coordinates."

"Coordinates for a location?"

"Exactly."

"Don't just stand there with that annoying grin on your face. Where's the location?"

"Golden Gate Bridge."

Sean swore and dropped into his chair. "Not possible. He's not going to commit a murder at the bridge—too many cameras."

"He dumped a body there."

"He was obviously aware of the cameras." Sean kicked his feet onto his desk and crossed his arms behind his head. "He kept out of their range. He's not going to kill at the bridge."

Curtis tugged on his ear. "Then why put down those coordinates in the message? If you're right, he told us he was going to kill two people on today's date. Makes sense he'd tell us where."

"He's toying with us. Don't expect logic from him or any real clues to his actions."

"You know more about that than I do." Curtis parked his cup on the blotter on Sean's desk and put a finger to his lips. "Did you catch Lopez's report on TV last night?"

"What of it?" Sean smiled through clenched teeth.

Curtis blinked and glanced over his shoulder. "The brass doesn't want the detective to become the story."

"Duh. Tell me something I don't already know."

"I'm just telling you to watch your back, bro." Curtis scurried off, his hands wrapped around his third mug of coffee for the day.

With the blood pounding against his temples, Sean tapped his keyboard to bring his computer to life. That was the second warning that he'd been issued this morning by well-meaning friends. How many not-so-well-meaning friends were out there spreading rumors and gossip?

When the search engine glowed brightly from the computer screen, Sean typed in the name Marie had given him earlier. He swiveled the monitor to the left, dragging it closer to the edge of the desk. If the brass could see what he was doing right now, they wouldn't be too thrilled about this, either.

It would be easier to use the police database to look up Dr. Patrick, but Sean didn't want to leave any kind of trail of his activities. He'd have to get his info like everyone else. A few papers Dr. Patrick had written about post-traumatic stress disorder popped up in the results, as well his attendance at a charitable organization's fund-raiser several years ago, but Sean couldn't get a line on a current location or phone number. Maybe he'd moved after his retirement.

His phone buzzed and his heart skipped a beat when he saw Elise's name on the display. "Everything okay?"

"Besides the fact that two of my students decided it was a good idea to color off the paper and onto the desktop, everything's good. Any news about that third set of numbers?"

"Longitude and latitude coordinates for the Golden Gate Bridge."

Elise sucked in some air. "That's the *where.*"

"It could've been if it were any other location, but the bridge? He can't think he's going to get away with murder on the bridge with the cameras up there."

"You have a point, but he avoided the cameras before when he dumped Katie's body."

"I think he's just messing with us…me."

"He seems to know your past, for sure." She coughed as the sound of kids floated over the line. "Did you get the name of the therapist?"

"Dr. James Patrick." He tapped his screen as if she could see it. "Just doing a search on him now but not having much luck. I could do better if I used my department resources and connections, but I don't want to go there right now."

She paused. "The department wouldn't be happy about you digging around in this stuff?"

He lowered his voice. "Apparently, they're already ticked off about Ray Lopez's report last night on the news."

"That's not your fault. You didn't ask him to dredge up ancient history."

The passion in her voice made his lip twitch—as if she were advocating for one of her kindergarteners. It had been a long time since he'd had an advocate.

"I can't change the past. Lopez has a right to delve into any story he wants. That's his job."

"I don't like reporters, never have."

"Is that because they made the runaway bride a three-day wonder back in Deer Loop, Montana?"

"It was longer than three days—must've been a slow week for news."

"Isn't every week a slow week for news in Deer Loop?"

She laughed and the noise over the line grew louder. "The bell just rang. I have to go back to class. Talk to you later?"

"Sure. Stay safe."

"You, too."

Sean held the phone to his ear a minute longer, listening to silence. It felt good to have someone in his corner—not that his brothers weren't. But they were younger when tragedy struck the family. It hadn't impacted them as much as him, and he'd wanted it that way.

After Mom had descended into a haze of booze and prescription drugs, he'd taken it upon himself to shield and protect his younger brothers.

Now, apparently, Elise had taken it upon herself to protect him. Not that there was much she could do, but yeah, it felt good.

He didn't want to start getting used to it.

ELISE SLASHED A red crayon across the neon green construction paper. "I will owe you big-time if you can find him for me."

Courtney tsked over the phone, but Elise could hear the click of her keyboard. "He's the cop. He can't get this info on his own?"

"He's doing this as a private citizen and doesn't want to use the department's resources." Elise held her breath as Courtney hummed across the line.

"Found him in one of my directories. No phone number, but I have an address for Dr. James Patrick and he's still local. Are you ready?"

"Fire away." Elise scribbled down the address as Courtney read it over the line. "Thank you so much."

"Just remember if things turn ugly, you didn't get this info from me."

Elise's belly fluttered. "Why would things turn ugly? Sean's a cop who needs some information from Dr. Patrick."

"Whatever you say, but be careful."

"Be careful? With Sean?" She'd never felt safer in her life than standing in the circle of that man's arms.

"I saw Lopez's report last night on the news, Elise. Don't you think it's kinda creepy?"

"The fact that his father was set up to take the fall for a string of murders? Yeah, really creepy."

Courtney cleared her throat. "The fact that Brody senior was suspected of being a serial killer and then he took the fall all right—right off the Golden Gate Bridge. And now his son is involved in a similar scenario? Creepy."

Anger, as hot as the red crayon, flashed through her body. "Sean is not creepy."

"No, I'd say Sean is a hot, sexy cop. But he might be a hot, sexy cop with a secret."

"He told me everything."

"After not telling you anything."

"Courtney…"

"I'm just asking you to be careful." She clicked her tongue. "I gotta go. That new client is on the other line."

Courtney ended the call, and Elise ripped the square containing Dr. Patrick's address from the construction paper.

Her friend was right. Sean had kept the whole truth from her, but then what did he owe her? The past had been Sean's personal affair until Ray Lopez had spilled the beans.

Yeah, just like Ty's woman on the side had been *his* personal affair.

The two situations weren't comparable. Ty's secret directly affected her, while Sean's was peripheral to the case. A homicide detective wasn't expected to divulge his personal history to a witness…or buy her dinner, or kiss her.

She dusted her fingers together and reached for her phone again. Sean's phone rang until it tripped over to his voice mail. "Sean, it's Elise. I got the address of Dr. Patrick, and he's still in the city. Call me when you get this message. I'm just leaving school now."

The rap on her door made her jump.

The uniformed cop held up his hands. "Sorry I startled you, Ms. Duran, but the older classes are getting dismissed early today and the school's going to be deserted soon."

"Thanks for the reminder. I'm on my way out."

"I'll wait for you."

True to his word, the officer waited and walked her out to her car. She waved as she pulled out of the school's parking lot.

As her car rolled off the Bay Bridge and into the city, Elise pulled to the side of the road and checked her phone. Still no response from Sean. She called and got his voice mail again. This time she left the doctor's address.

She maneuvered through the city streets and realized the doctor lived on the way to Courtney's. Maybe she should swing by his place and scope it out for Sean.

Courtney would probably be tied up with her pesky new client, and Elise didn't want to rush home to an empty place. She'd had enough of empty places.

Cupping her phone in her hand, she read Dr. Patrick's address aloud. The phone responded and intoned directions to the location.

Elise turned onto Dr. Patrick's street and squinted out her window at the addresses on the row of town houses. She located his address in brass numbers on the outside of a beige stucco building and rolled to a stop at the curb.

Before turning off the engine, she glanced at the clock on the dashboard. Then she plucked her phone from the cup holder and scrolled through her messages—nothing from Sean.

She punched in the number for the station, and a woman answered the phone.

"SFPD Homicide."

"Hello, I'm trying to reach Detective Brody. Is he in today?"

"He's been in a meeting all afternoon. Can I take a message?"

"No, that's okay. I already left him a message on his cell phone."

"He'll get it when the meeting's over, since they usually turn off their cell phones in there."

"Okay, thanks." Elise tapped the edge of her phone against her chin. Should she wait for Sean or just go to Courtney's? He'd piqued her curiosity with that story about his father. What a tragic chain of events.

If Sean's father had been innocent of the crimes, it was all for nothing. *If?* Sean was convinced his father had been innocent, but what child wouldn't believe that of a beloved father?

Her eyes strayed to the front of Dr. Patrick's town house. Would the doctor be able to shed any light on the truth? Even if he implicated Sean's father, would Sean believe him? And if he did implicate Sean's father, would Sean admit that to her?

She gripped the door handle. What did it matter? This was Sean's business.

She folded her hands in her lap. But it wasn't just Sean's

business anymore. There was a killer out there who knew all about Sean's history, a killer who had her in his crosshairs.

After that fiasco with Ty, she'd vowed never to be kept in the dark again, and this situation with Sean was a lot darker than a cheating fiancé.

She grabbed the door handle again and pushed out of the car before she could talk herself out of it. Pausing on the steps to the town house, she pulled out her phone and left another message for Sean letting him know her plans.

She might not want to be kept in the dark, but she didn't want to keep him in the dark, either.

With just fourteen units in the building, Elise located Dr. Patrick's place quickly. A sliding window beside the front door was open halfway across, and the sounds of a game show floated through the mesh screen obscuring the view inside the house.

She scooped in a deep breath and rang the doorbell.

A bump and a scrape resounded from inside, and Elise straightened her shoulders and plastered a smile on her face as if this were the most natural house call in the world. But the door didn't swing open.

She knocked, leaning in toward the window. "Dr. Patrick? My name is Elise Duran. I'm a friend of Detective Sean Brody's. He…we wanted to ask you a few questions about his father, Detective Joseph Brody."

The scraping noise grew louder, and a raspy moan accompanied it.

"Dr. Patrick?" Elise pressed her face against the screen.

A man, leaning heavily against a kitchen chair, shuffled toward the door, one hand holding his left arm.

Elise's stomach flip-flopped. "Dr. Patrick? Are you all right?"

She jiggled the door handle. Another loud scrape and a bump, and then the handle turned. The door opened inward, and the man hunched over in the doorway, his face contorted, a line of drool running from his mouth.

The chair bumped Elise's knees and she realized he was using it as a walker.

"Are you okay?" She placed a knee on the chair. "I'm calling 9-1-1."

Dr. Patrick let out a gasp and toppled to the side.

Elise shoved the useless chair out of the way and crouched beside him, reaching for her phone with a shaky hand. "It's going to be all right. I'm calling 9-1-1 right now."

He clutched her wrist in a cinching vise and pulled her toward him as the phone dropped from her hand. His mouth was working and his dark eyes burned into hers. He strained to keep his chin to his chest, holding his head off the floor.

She ducked, her ear hovering close to his mouth while she felt for her phone on the hardwood floor.

His words rasped from his throat. "Tell him, tell Brody."

Elise's jaw dropped and she froze. "Tell him what?"

"Tell him, tell him…his father…"

Dr. Patrick's eyes rolled to the back of his head and he slumped to the floor.

Chapter Thirteen

As the fog rolled in damp and heavy, Sean narrowed his eyes and watched the EMTs load the gurney burdened with Dr. Patrick's body into the ambulance.

Elise's shoulder pressed against his, and he felt a tremble roll through her slender frame. He took a step to the side. "What the hell were you thinking?"

Her head swiveled around so fast, her hair whipped across her face. A few strands stuck to her damp cheeks. "I didn't cause his heart attack."

"I didn't accuse of you of causing his…heart attack, but what were you doing coming out to his place on your own?" That fact upset him more than the idea that she obviously didn't trust him.

"I was driving back to Courtney's from school. It's not like I have a police escort. I could've stopped off for groceries, dropped in on a friend."

"But you chose to come here."

"Look—" she splayed her hands in front of her "—I had Dr. Patrick's address, you were busy and I happened to be in the neighborhood."

He shoved his hands in his pockets as the ambulance trundled away from the curb. No need for a siren—Dr. Patrick was already dead from the heart attack.

"Why didn't you wait for me? Or why did you have to

wait at all? You left me his address. I could've handled the questioning on my own." He started to shake a finger in her face and made a fist instead.

"Maybe it was fate that propelled me to go in on my own. By the time you got here, he would've been dead."

"I guess fate's not looking out for you too well, since by the time you got here he was dying."

She held up her own finger. "Dying, not dead."

"What does that mean?" He hadn't had two minutes to talk to her alone. By the time he got her message and had driven to Dr. Patrick's address, the cops had already been here and he'd arrived to see the tail end of their patrol car. The EMTs were already wheeling Dr. Patrick out of his town house, and Elise was talking to the neighbors, who were now wandering back to their own lives.

He had no idea what she'd told the cops about her reasons for being here. Had she dragged his name into it?

"It means—" she brushed the hair from her face "—he wasn't dead when I got here. He'd already suffered the heart attack but he was still alive."

"How long did he last?"

"Long enough to talk to me."

He scuffed the toe of his shoe against the sidewalk. "What would he have to say to a complete stranger?"

"I wouldn't say I was a complete stranger." She flicked a piece of lint from the arm of her sweater. "I told him who I was through the window."

"You mentioned my name?"

"Yes."

"What did he say?" Sean sucked in a breath and held it.

She hugged her sweater around her body. "He told me to tell you something about your father."

His lips barely moved in his stiff face. "What?"

"He died before he could tell me."

Sean let out a noisy breath that deflated his chest along

with his hopes. "He knew, Elise. He knew something about my father."

She placed her cool fingers on his arm. "If he knew enough to clear your father, why didn't he step forward at the time? I'm pretty sure your father would've allowed him to break confidentiality to vouch for his innocence."

"Are you implying Dr. Patrick knew my father was guilty?"

"No." Her fingernails dug into his tattoo. "I'm just trying to reason through this with you."

He shook his head. "There is no rhyme or reason. Why did Dr. Patrick have a heart attack today of all days, just when I found out about his existence?"

"Coincidence. Fate, again. It was a heart attack, not murder, not suicide."

"The EMTs verified that to you?"

"Short of doing an autopsy on the sidewalk? Pretty much."

"Damn! Minutes too late. Minutes away from getting to the bottom of this puzzle that has plagued me for twenty years."

Her hold on his arm turned to a caress. "The puzzle, as you call it, doesn't define you, Sean. Whatever your father was or did, you're here now, in this moment."

The tension seeped from his shoulders and he rolled them forward and backward. Then he clasped her hands between his.

She wriggled one free from his tight grip and brushed her knuckles across his tattoo. "And you know it. That's what this is about, isn't it? You're a Phoenix. You've risen from the ashes of your past to create your own present."

As always, he shivered when she touched his tattoo, as if she were touching his soul. "Let's get out of here and get something to eat."

"That sounds great about now, but I don't want you to

get into any trouble because of me. Does your department have any idea you're spending so much time with me?"

Sean clutched the back of his neck to knead his tense muscles. In all the worry about Elise and the drama over Dr. Patrick's death, he'd almost forgotten the meeting this afternoon. "That's not going to be a problem."

"Are you sure?"

"It's not going to be a problem because I'm no longer on the case. It's happening again, Elise."

ELISE STEPPED BACK and placed a hand on her car. "Your department took you off the case? Why?"

"The captain thinks I'm too personally involved." He held up one finger. "And before you get started, it has nothing to do with you."

"It was that reporter's story, wasn't it? Dragging up the past."

He shrugged. "Like I said before, he has a right to report whatever he wants as long as it's the truth—and he told the truth. The department overreacted."

"Sean, what did you mean when you said it was happening again? They don't suspect you of anything, do they?"

"I just meant—" he dug his keys out of his pocket "—they're punishing me because some killer decided to communicate with me. That's how it started with my dad, too."

"Well, it's not going to end the same way."

He reached forward and tugged a lock of her damp hair. "Why are we standing out here in this fog? Follow me back to my place and I'll make some dinner. It's just outside the city, if you don't mind."

"Perfect. I want to get out of the city right now, but I don't want to put you to any trouble. Let me pick up the food this time."

She'd clicked her remote and he opened the car door

for her. "I actually have a couple of steaks in the freezer I've been meaning to cook for a while."

"Then I'll take you up on your offer."

"Stay right behind me and I'll keep my eye on you, but just in case." He printed out his address on a piece of paper and slipped it into her hand. He shut her door and smacked the roof of the car.

Keeping her gaze pinned to the taillights of his car had the same effect on her as watching him in her rearview mirror—a feeling of safety. After Dr. Patrick died in her arms and the ambulance arrived and the police came, she hadn't felt safe until she'd seen Sean striding across the street, his gait fueled by fury. His fury fueled by fear.

He cared about her. Whether his concern extended beyond feelings of protectiveness, she didn't know. Did it matter right now? She needed his strength and he needed hers, too.

He'd been fighting his demons for far too long by himself. He obviously didn't want to burden his brothers. He had no one right now to confide in, and she knew how that felt.

When the expectations of her small-town life began to close around her, she didn't know where to turn. So she'd gone through the motions, treading the path that had been laid out for her.

When her maid of honor had dangled the gift of Ty's infidelity in front of her, she'd snatched it. She knew once she became that runaway bride, there was no going back.

Maybe Sean needed something to hold on to, something to pull him out of his misery. He must've turned a corner when he got that tattoo. Now she'd been put here to help him turn another corner.

She followed him closely on the bumper-to-bumper freeway until he put his turn signal on and crawled onto an off-ramp. As she rolled to a stop behind him at the red light, she tapped the display of her phone to call Courtney.

"Hi, Elise. Are you calling because you're going to be late? Because I'm not even home yet."

"I'm going out to dinner, or rather having dinner at a friend's place."

"Turns out I'm going out, too. I'm finally getting together with the guy I met at the Speakeasy."

A shiver ran through Elise. Courtney should be more careful. "What do you know about this guy, Courtney?"

"Uh, he's an investment banker and he's hot."

Elise grimaced. Her experiences over the past few days had made her more street savvy than she'd wanted to be.

"Are you at home yet?"

"No. New client's keeping me busy. Have fun and be careful."

Elise pressed her lips together. She didn't want to tell Courtney about her latest mishap. "You, too."

Ahead of her, Sean's right-turn signal blinked and he swung into the driveway of a small house in a quiet residential neighborhood. He must relish this escape from the big city.

He parked in the driveway and she pulled up to the curb.

Tossing his keys in the air, he said, "Miserable traffic."

"This is a nice neighborhood."

"Yeah, my little refuge."

"You need it."

He unlocked his front door and shoved it open for her. "Don't get me wrong. I love my job."

"I know you do. You wouldn't be babysitting me if you didn't."

He tilted his head as he stepped aside, a quizzical look in his dark eyes. "Right."

She stepped into the room and inhaled the scent of cleanliness—furniture polish, bleach, disinfectant.

"It's a good thing my cleaning lady came today." He flipped on a lamp by the door, and it illuminated a masculine room, dark and cozy.

She placed her hands on the back of his couch, smoothing them across the dark brown leather. "Somehow I get the feeling your cleaning lady doesn't have a lot of work to do."

"How much mess can a single guy create?" He spread his arms to encompass the immaculate room.

"You don't know my brothers." She pointed at the kitchen, whose gleaming surfaces were visible even in the darkness. "Do you want me to help with anything?"

"Sure. I'm going to thaw out the steaks and put a couple of potatoes in microwave. I have some fresh asparagus from the local farmers' market. You can wash and trim that."

She saluted. "Got it."

As he covered the steaks on a plate and shoved them into the microwave, Elise ran some cold water over the asparagus spears. "What did they tell you when they dismissed you from the case?"

His fingers paused over the microwave buttons, and then he stabbed them and punched the power. "Said they didn't like killers communicating with detectives, that the killers fed off the high and it could encourage them to commit more murders."

"You obviously don't believe that."

"When a killer communicates with the detective on the case, it tends to yield more clues. There are more chances that he'll slip up, reveal some detail." He grabbed a couple of potatoes from the pantry and slammed the door. "They know that."

"So, it's just you."

"Yeah, it's me. If the killer had chosen anyone else in the department, they'd be all over it."

"Do you think he will?" She took a potato from his hands and held it under the running water. "Replace you with another detective?"

He snorted. "Not a chance. He's fixated on me for some reason—probably because he knows all about my father. He's not exactly a copycat of that killer, but he's close enough. Thinks he's being clever by pulling another Brody into his sick world."

She bit her lip. "No news on anything happening at the bridge today at those coordinates he sent me?"

"No. Those coordinates were for my edification. Who knows what he has planned next, if anything."

He snatched the potato from her, which she'd been scrubbing down to the flesh. "I like a little potato skin on my baked potatoes."

She laughed. "Crime and cooking don't mix."

"Crime and a lot of things don't mix. Let's drop it."

They finished preparing the meal by exchanging small talk, and it almost felt like a normal date. But she'd never dated anyone like Sean Brody before. His intensity always simmered beneath the surface. He ran so hot, he could grill those steaks without the heat.

She stole a glance at his backside, snug in a pair of faded jeans he'd pulled on after shedding his suit. What would it feel like to have all that intensity unleashed in the bedroom?

"Rare or well-done?"

"Huh?" She blinked as he shot her a curious glance over his shoulder.

"Your steak—rare, medium or well-done?"

"I grew up on a cattle ranch. I like mine medium rare and juicy."

His eyes flicked to her chest and back to her face so quickly she might have imagined it. "Juicy, it is."

She dug into his silverware drawer and grabbed a handful of utensils. Had he read her thoughts? Probably just looked at her face, which would forever preclude her from being a professional poker player.

The microwave beeped and he turned from the sizzling steaks. "That's your asparagus. I have some butter over here, unless you prefer something fancier."

"I prefer…butter." She turned and grabbed the bowl of asparagus from the microwave and felt like replacing it with her head. If that's the best she could do at seduction, the only beef she'd get tonight would be that medium-rare steak. She giggled. She'd been hanging around Courtney too long.

"Something funny about the asparagus?"

"Well, there is something inherently funny about the vegetable, isn't there." She plucked a hot spear from the bowl with her fingertips and held it up. "It even looks like a…"

She bit off the end of the asparagus and practically choked on it.

Sean cleared his throat. "Phallic symbol?"

Popping the rest of the spear in her mouth, she nodded. She should've been paying more attention to Courtney over the past year of their friendship. She was pretty sure her friend wouldn't be using asparagus as a tool of seduction.

Sean stabbed the steaks with a long fork and dropped them onto two plates. "I think I got that medium rare. Let me know your expert opinion."

"Actually, I've probably had one steak since hightailing it out of Montana."

"Uh-oh. Is this steak going to bring up bad memories and make you head for the hills?"

"I think I can handle it. Steak sauce?"

"In the fridge."

He stood by his chair until she sat down across from him. "We make a good team…in the kitchen."

She took a gulp of water. She had to get out of dangerous territory. Clutching her fork and steak knife, she said, "I think we make a pretty good investigative team, too. Is there any way we can unseal Dr. Patrick's files now that he's dead?"

Sean didn't seem to mind the shift in topic, and his brow furrowed as he cut into his steak. "That's what's been bothering me, one of many things. If the department knew my father was seeing Dr. Patrick at the time of his…death, I would've thought they'd demand his records."

"Maybe they did."

"But they left everything as unsolved. Those murders are still cold cases. If Dr. Patrick's sessions with my father had proved his innocence or guilt, it would've come out."

"Did you ever ask anyone?"

"I wasn't aware that my father even saw Dr. Patrick until we discussed it this morning." He put down his fork with a piece of meat stuck to the end, a frown still marring his features.

"What is it?"

"Don't you think it's an incredible coincidence that the day I discover Dr. Patrick saw my father, the good doctor winds up dropping dead of a heart attack?"

"Yes, especially since he died at my feet. But what are you saying? A heart attack is a heart attack. Do you think my visit caused his heart attack?" She ran crisscrosses on her plate with her fork.

"Seems like he suffered the attack just before you arrived."

"What's your point, Sean?"

"Heart attacks can be induced."

She dropped her fork. "You think someone killed Dr. Patrick by injecting him with something that caused his heart to fail?"

"It's too coincidental, Elise. It's unbelievable that his death occurred the very day we found him."

"And it's believable that someone killed him? Why would someone want to kill Dr. Patrick before he could tell you anything about your father?"

"I don't know, but I'm going to find out." He picked up his fork and took the piece of steak between his teeth.

"If you don't believe your father had anything to do with those murders twenty years ago and he was never formally charged or convicted, does it really matter anymore? You *are* secure in your beliefs, aren't you?"

He chewed, swallowed, took a sip of water and gazed over her shoulder. Then his eyes tracked back to her face, and she saw the doubt in their depths. "Maybe that's it, Elise."

She had to hunch forward to catch his words, and she caught his hand at the same time. "It's okay to have that uncertainty, Sean. It's not being disloyal. You were a kid at the time."

"I don't want to believe it." He twisted his fingers around hers. "The man who taught me everything, the man I looked up to, couldn't be a cold-blooded killer. He would've had to have been a complete sociopath." Without losing his hold on her hand, he slumped back in his chair. "That's the scary part. I know they exist. I know there are people out there who act just like you and me—who love and laugh and feel pain—but it's all a pretense. They feel nothing at all."

"It's more than just proving your father's innocence to the world. You have to prove it to yourself. I get that."

"How did we get here?" He loosened his grip on her fingers and traced her knuckles with the pad of one finger. "You have a killer sending you notes, launching sneak attacks and you just had a man die at your feet. And you're trying to make me feel better."

"You've done more than enough, more than I ever expected from that moment you sat down next to me in the emergency room. You've been by my side, going beyond the call of duty to protect me." She shrugged her shoulders. "I'm just paying you back."

He lifted one eyebrow. "Is that what you think this is all about? Protection? Securing a witness?"

The pulse in her wrist ticked up several notches. Could he feel it? "I'm the only witness you have right now."

He chuckled in the back of his throat, and the low sound sent a line of tingles racing down to her toes.

"The SFPD is not in the bodyguarding business. We're not going to put you in the Witness Protection Program. It's not like you have the goods on a mobster or anything." He scooted his chair back and tossed his napkin onto the table. "Everything I've done for you has been off the books and off the clock."

She twisted her own napkin in her lap as she tilted her head back to take in his imposing figure. "Why'd you do it?"

"Do you have to ask?" He dropped into a crouch in front of her, like a beast ready to pounce. "You may be a kindergarten teacher from Podunk, Montana, but you're also the runaway bride. You're the woman in my kitchen waving around asparagus and talking about juicy slabs of meat."

She choked. "I…I…"

In one fluid movement, he rose to his full height, catching her under the arms and taking her with him. He supported the back of her head with one hand and pulled her close with an arm wrapped around her waist.

He stared into her face, his lips centimeters from her own, so close she felt the scorching heat of his breath. "I want you, Elise Duran. I've wanted you from the minute I saw you bundled up in that hospital bed, and I can't even explain it."

Her breath came out in short spurts. "Maybe I'm your redemption, the means of redressing your father's sins."

"If redemption feels this good—" he ran a slow hand down the beads of her spine and rested it on the curve of her hip "—I should've gone in for it years ago."

Her lashes fluttered and she parted her lips. If he released her now, she'd fall to the floor.

"Now stop." He kissed her temple. "Talking." He kissed her left eyelid. "About." He kissed her earlobe. "My father." His lips trailed across her throat, and his tongue circled the indentation below her Adam's apple.

She slid her hands beneath his T-shirt and caressed the muscles of his back. Goose bumps raced across his smooth skin in response to her touch.

He nibbled her collarbone, sweeping the hair from her neck. His lips followed along its curve while he hooked a finger beneath her bra strap and top to bare her shoulder. "Your skin is so soft, like the petal of a rose."

She'd imagined making love to Sean many times in the past few days, but she never expected poetry from him.

Her head dropped to the side, and her legs trembled. A very soft sigh escaped from her lips.

He growled in her ear. "I'm not going to take you here among the asparagus."

He was going to *take* her? Before she could process that thought, he swept her off her feet. "Allow me to show you the rest of the house, or at least the most important room."

"You mean the kitchen isn't the most important room in the house?" She dug her fingers into his thick dark hair.

"Only for asparagus."

She buried her face in his warm neck as he carried her to the back of the house. He bumped open a door and she balanced her chin on his shoulder to take in the view. The large bed, low to the floor, dominated the room with black lacquer pieces lining the walls.

He put her down on the throw rug by the side of the bed, and she placed one foot on the mattress. "At least you don't have to worry about falling out of this thing."

"It's a Japanese-style bed frame. Do you want to analyze my furniture or finish what we started?"

She curled her fingers in the belt loops of his jeans and tugged him toward her. "I have an idea. Let's analyze the furniture first, starting with the bed."

Encircling his hands around her waist, he bent his knees and brought her down with him until they were kneeling face-to-face, the low mattress behind her. He dropped his hands and cupped her derriere beneath her thin skirt.

His kiss cut off her breath and sent her heart racing. Everything about him had seemed so hard, but his lips felt soft and supple. His tongue traced the seam of her mouth and she opened it to the demanding pressure.

One hand had bunched up her skirt and she gasped when his rough hand brushed across the silky material of her panties, catching the soft material on the pads of his fingers.

He nudged her down on the bed, and the mattress conformed to her weight and then his as he stretched out beside her. He lifted her blouse, pulling it over her head. He followed the edge of her lacy bra with the tip of his tongue.

Thank goodness she'd donned some good underwear this morning before she'd left for school—about twelve hours ago. Before she'd been chasing kindergartners on the playground and finger-painting with them. Before some stranger died in her lap.

"Wait." She struggled up, propping herself up on her elbows.

His eyes popped open. "You're not going to run, are you?"

She rolled off the bed. "I'd like to take a shower, if that's okay."

"That's fine." With a deft touch, he reached behind her and unzipped her skirt. "But don't think I'm letting you go in there alone."

"Of course not." She gulped, and when she got up from the bed, she left her skirt behind her.

Sean peeled off his shirt and tossed it over his shoulder. When he stood up, he touched a finger to her nose. "You have the best ideas."

She drank in what he'd been hiding under his button-up shirts and tailored jackets. His tattoo snaked up his arm, curling around his biceps. Slabs of hard muscle shifted across his broad chest as he reached down to unbutton his fly.

She swallowed and held her breath. Her friends in Montana had warned her that all she'd find in San Francisco was citified metrosexuals. If they could see her now—or rather see Sean.

Not wanting to appear greedy, her gaze returned to his face as he peeled his jeans from his hips. A quick glance downward confirmed he'd shed his briefs along with his jeans.

He reached out and pulled her against his naked body. She closed her eyes and let out a long breath.

"Why are you still wearing so many clothes?" His fingers fumbled with her bra, and in a matter of seconds they were skin to skin, their bodies meeting along every line.

"That's better." He kissed her mouth and then left her lips throbbing and wanting as he pressed kisses along her throat. Every spot he touched seemed to alight in fire.

She choked out, "Shower."

Taking her hand, he led her to the attached bathroom and cranked on the water in the tiled shower. Water streamed from two showerheads.

She stepped into the warm spray and he joined her. He squirted some liquid soap in the palm of his hand and rubbed his hands together. "Now, what is it that needs washing so much that you had to interrupt my flow in the bedroom?"

She dragged her gaze away from the water sluicing over the planes of his body. "Everywhere."

"I was hoping you'd say that." He flashed her a grin that had her groping for the shower wall for support.

His warm hands, slick with soap, started at her shoulders and quickly descended to her breasts, where he circled her nipples, teasing and provoking them.

His palms rubbed her belly, and she couldn't help the moan that escaped her lips.

"Turn around." His hands cinched her waist and he spun her around toward the bench that extended from the shower wall.

He shifted his attention from her stomach to her inner thighs, and she parted her legs as the spray of water hit her shoulder.

He nudged her from behind, urging her to bend over, his erection spearing her lower back.

She placed her palms flat on the bench beaded with water.

Sean cupped one hand between her legs, and her hips automatically swiveled. She panted. "I thought this was supposed to be a shower."

"And I'm very thorough in my cleaning. Don't want to miss one little spot." His soapy fingers caressed her flesh, and her arms began to shake.

He moved rhythmically against her, his hard, tight erection probing between her open legs. His magic fingers continued their exploration of her throbbing folds. When he entered her with first one finger and then a second, she closed around him.

He cupped her breast, pinching her nipple, and then his

teeth nipped the back of her neck. The contrasting sensations overwhelmed her senses and she exploded.

As she rode the wave of her release, he plunged into her from behind. He was delivering all the intensity that had been simmering beneath the surface. She'd wondered what it would be like unleashed, and now she knew. Overwhelming.

Every time he entered her, he took her to some new height, some realm inhabited by just the two of them. When he pulled out, she felt moments of pure desolation.

He reached between her legs again, and his touch was so electrifying she screamed. Within seconds her muscles tensed and she clenched her jaw. She was almost afraid of the power that gathered within her.

The gentleness of his touch contrasted with the force of his thrusts inside her, and once again she broke. The pleasure that flooded her body melted her and she sobbed, pressing her wet face against her arm.

He whispered her name over and over and it echoed in the shower, surrounding her as he surrounded her. He pounded against her, skin on skin, and when his climax came, it engulfed both of them in its ferocity.

No moaning, groaning or grunting for Sean. He howled. And the sound of his passion, of his possession of her, sent a thrill to her core.

When he spent himself inside her, he covered her with his body. His legs twined around hers, his arms wrapped around her torso, his chest and belly were sealed against her back to the juncture where their bodies remained connected in the most intimate way.

The lukewarm water beat against their entwined forms as they gasped for breath. Slowly, he peeled away from her and slipped out of her. She felt the loss of him in the pit of her stomach, so she straightened and turned in one movement and clung to his chest.

He smoothed the damp hair from her face. "I'm sorry. Did I hurt you? I couldn't...couldn't help myself."

Then she realized tears, not just water, were coursing down her cheeks.

She nuzzled against his chest, the sprinkling of dark hair ticking her nose. "You have nothing to be sorry about. You just took me somewhere, someplace—" she dug her fingernails in his firm buttocks "—I don't know."

He chuckled and wedged a knuckle beneath her chin, tilting her head back. "Would it be too cliché to say 'paradise'?"

"You felt it, too?" She rubbed the water from her eyes.

"You're kidding, right?" He cupped her face in his hands. "Do you think it's every day I howl at the moon during sex?"

The happiness that welled in her chest overcame her, and tears sprang to her eyes again.

He kissed one of her eyelids. "If you keep crying, I'm going to think I'm a brute."

She slapped his chest with her hand. "Are you kidding? Do you think it's every day I break down and cry during sex?"

The smile dropped from his face, and his dark eyes kindled. "It was special, wasn't it? I don't generally go in for the mushy stuff, but you make me feel...mushy."

Her fingers traced the ridges of his pecs. "You don't feel mushy at all."

"You just ruined my mushy moment." He smacked her backside. "Let's get out of here before we both look like prunes."

Sean tucked a towel around his waist and padded out of the bathroom, returning with a fresh towel for her.

He held it out for her as she stepped from the shower. "You do realize that if I towel you off, it's going to ignite that fire down below all over again."

She fluttered her lashes. “Is that a threat or a promise?”

He wrapped the towel around her body. “You do have school tomorrow, right? You don’t want to come in with a sex hangover.”

“I don’t know.” She dropped the towel. “Is that the kind of hangover that can be cured with the hair of the dog?”

Sean made a move but stopped when his cell phone rang in the bedroom. “Oops, that’s my work phone. I’d better pick that up, but hold that thought.”

She gathered her towel from the floor and followed him into the bedroom. He was right. She had to get it together and return to Courtney’s to get ready for school. They’d have another chance to be together. Wouldn’t they?

Despite being half-naked, Sean had already morphed back into the dedicated cop with the phone call. He sat on the edge of the bed, the cell pressed to his ear, his face creased into lines of worry. “Uh-huh. Uh-huh. Do you think I asked him to contact me? Do you think I want it?”

A sick feeling twisted her gut, and she edged out of the bedroom, tucking a corner of the towel in the edge at her chest. She couldn’t take any more, not after what they’d just shared. She wasn’t ready to crash to earth just yet.

She wandered into the kitchen and collected the plates from the table while Sean’s voice rumbled from the other room. As she ran water over the dishes, someone pounded on Sean’s front door.

She dropped the silverware in the sink with a clatter and grabbed a dish towel, twisting it in front of her on the way to the door.

Sean stalked out of the bedroom, clutching his phone in his fist. “Who the hell is that?”

Elise reached the door before he did and peered through the peephole. Her heart galloped in her chest as she fumbled with the dead bolt.

“Wait, Elise. What are you doing?”

"It's Ty." She yanked at the door. "And he's hurt."

"What?"

She got the door open and Ty stumbled into the room, his face battered and pale, a white T-shirt, seeping blood, wrapped thickly around one hand.

She caught him in midstagger and he almost took her down. "Ty, what is it? What happened to you?"

He raised the hand swaddled in the bloody T-shirt and aimed it at Sean. "He happened to me. His henchman attacked me, and then the SOB chopped off my finger. He took my finger."

Ty collapsed face-first on the floor.

Chapter Fourteen

Elise's face took on a shade of green as she swayed over Ty collapsed at her feet.

Sean didn't need two unconscious people on his floor. He took Elise's arm and led her to a chair. "Sit."

Crouching over Ty, he punched in 9-1-1 on the phone still clutched in his hand. He unwound the stained T-shirt from Ty's hand and swore at the bloody mess. He'd been telling the truth about one thing—someone had hacked off his left ring finger.

Why had the idiot come here instead of calling 9-1-1 or driving himself to an emergency room?

"I-is he okay?"

"Passed out from a loss of blood."

"His finger?"

"Gone."

"Oh, my God. Oh, my God." Elise bounded from the chair, but Sean held out his hand.

"Sit down, Elise. There's nothing you can do for him. The ambulance is on its way."

She plopped back down on the chair, knotting her fingers. "Why? What happened? Who did this?"

Given Ty's missing finger, Sean had a clue but Elise didn't need to hear it right now. "If you want to help, bring me a clean dish towel from the kitchen…and my pants."

She looked down at her own towel slipping from her body and jumped up once again. She headed into the kitchen first and returned to the living room, tossing a terry-cloth towel at him. While he loosened the T-shirt from Ty's hand and replaced it with the towel, binding it tightly around the gaping wound, Elise disappeared down the hallway.

Back in her skirt and sweater, she dropped his jeans beside him. He looked up. "If you're feeling up to it, can you hold this towel in place for a few seconds?"

Nodding, she curled her legs beneath her and sat next to Ty.

Sean placed her hands around the towel. "Squeeze as hard as you can."

He yanked on his jeans and tossed the bath towel aside. He squatted next to her and nudged her hands away from the makeshift bandage staunching the flow of Ty's blood.

She slumped back, her hands falling in her lap. "Why did this happen, Sean? This can't be a coincidence."

"I don't think it is." She'd realize just how unlikely a coincidence if she found out about Katie Duncan's finger.

Sirens wailed down the street. "Can you go outside and meet them? I phoned it in, but tell them he lost a finger and a lot of blood."

Elise scrambled outside, and minutes later the EMTs bustled through the front door with a gurney. They peppered Sean with questions as they loaded up Ty.

As they wheeled Ty to the ambulance, one of the EMTs called over his shoulder, "Do you know where the finger is?"

"Nope. Like I said, it didn't happen here." But if Sean could guess, it might be arriving in a package for him soon.

Officer Ashford, the cop who had been quietly talking to Elise, emerged onto the porch. "Can I ask you a few questions, Detective Brody?"

"Of course. Here? Back inside?"

"Here is fine." He jerked his pencil over his shoulder. "Ms. Duran said the victim blamed you for his attack, said you hired someone to assault him."

"Yeah, he did say that. I don't know why he believes that. He passed out before we could question him."

"What do you know about Ty Russell?"

"He's Elise's former fiancé, and he's here to convince her to go back to Montana with him. That's about it."

"And you and Elise are…friendly." Ashford's eyes flicked across Sean's bare chest.

His jaw clenched. "Yes."

Ashford tapped his pencil and licked his lips. "Elise Duran is the first victim of the Alphabet Killer. The case you just got pulled from."

"Yep." Sean folded his arms. If this pip-squeak patrolman thought he could intimidate him with his leading questions, he needed to go back to the academy.

"You haven't been too busy to know he struck again, have you?"

Elise gasped behind him. "Sean?"

"Captain Williams notified me just before Russell showed up on my doorstep." Out of the corner of his eye, he could see Elise creeping closer to him until he could feel the warmth of her presence on his skin.

The cop's face fell a little. Then he puffed out his chest again. "The two victims have last names beginning with C."

"Well, then I guess he's working backward through the alphabet, isn't he?"

"Those victims were also missing their fingers."

Elise sobbed behind him, and Sean lunged for the cop, grabbing the shirt of his uniform. He breathed heavily in Ashford's startled face. "You need to go back to school, son. That's privileged information about this case. We're not revealing that to the public."

Ashford wriggled out of Sean's grasp and stumbled backward off the porch. His face reddened and he blustered, "I'm reporting you, Brody. I may even have you arrested for assaulting a police officer. You detectives think you're something special. You're special, all right. You're neck deep with the Alphabet Killer. Hell, you may even *be* him. A killer—just like your old man."

Sean's eye twitched and his muscles coiled. He felt Elise's warm hand pressed against the small of his back.

He tilted his head back and forth to crack his neck, and then he said, "Whatever."

Turning his back on Ashford, his mouth still gaping, Sean took Elise's arm and pulled her into the house.

"Don't listen to him, Sean." She wrapped her arms around his waist, and his house never felt like such a home before.

He squeezed her tight. "What he says doesn't bother me. What bothers me is that the killer tracked down Ty, and we have two more dead bodies."

"It's awful." She hid her face against his chest. "Two people killed today on six, twelve. Wh-where were their bodies found?"

"Not on the Golden Gate Bridge, so those coordinates were just a tease. The bodies were found in the Bayview area."

"You were right. He was just toying with us." She leaned back to look into his face. "Who were they, Sean? Did Captain Williams tell you their names?"

"A man and a woman this time."

She closed her eyes and her lashes fluttered on her cheeks. "Was that cop right? Were their fingers missing?"

"Just like Katie Duncan's."

"You never told me that." Her nostrils flared as her eyes flew open.

"That was supposed to be confidential information. How that moron found out and why he's spreading it around, I don't have a clue. I'm no longer on the case, as he pointed out."

"Then why did Captain Williams call you at this time of night to tell you about the bodies?"

He left the circle of her arms and paced to the window to stare out at the dark street. "Because the killer left me another message."

"What was it this time?" She pressed her fingers against her lips.

"Elise…"

"Just tell me, Sean."

"He left me the same type of note that he left you at the school, but with slightly different numbers. They're working on it, but the location was a joke last time so we can't trust him."

Two vertical lines formed between her eyebrows. "Where did they find the note?"

He clasped the back of his neck and chewed on his lip. Did Elise really need the visual of a note wrapped around a severed finger and shoved into one of the victim's pockets? "He left a note on one of the bodies."

"What does he want with you?"

"I already know that. The bigger question is what does he want from you?" He tapped on the window with his fingernail. "How did he know about Ty? How did he know about you and me, about our spending time together?"

She knotted her fingers together. "I don't know. He didn't get all that from my purse, or from my house. He must've been the one who attacked Ty. He probably told Ty he was working for you. Where else would Ty get that crazy idea?"

"When Ty regains consciousness, we can ask him. Maybe he can give us a description. How did the guy even approach Ty?"

"It's like he's dancing around me, us. He's playing some kind of game with us that started the night he attacked me."

"And that game has its roots in the past, twenty years in the past." Sean blew out a breath, crossed the room and took Elise's hand. "I'm sorry the night had to end this way. I'm sorry about Ty."

"Me, too," she whispered, and tears welled in her eyes. "For a moment there we pushed it all away, didn't we? For a moment it was just the two of us."

He kissed her trembling lips. "It can be that way again, Elise. This will all be over soon."

She nodded, her eyes widening, and he had a feeling he'd just made a promise he wasn't sure he could keep. Would it ever be over for him? In his gut, he knew it would never be over until he found out what happened twenty years ago in this city.

He stroked her hair back from her face. "I'm going to get a shirt on and see you back home. You still have two more days of school to get through, right?"

"You don't have to follow me back. I'll head straight to Courtney's place and drive right into the garage. It's a secure building. I'll be fine."

He walked into the bedroom and pulled a clean T-shirt from his closet. Yanking it over his head, he returned to the living room and said, "I'm not comfortable with you driving alone at night. It's late."

He scratched the stubble of his beard. This whole incident with Ty Russell had spooked him. How the hell had the killer gotten a line on Ty?

As far as he knew, the only time Elise had seen Ty since he'd been in the city was the day he swooped down on her in front of Courtney's place. He hadn't seen his name in her phone contacts, and he doubted Elise had anything in her house with Ty's name on it.

"Well, I guess I could always use a police escort. I'm obviously not very good about noticing a tail since the Alphabet Killer managed to follow me from the Golden Gate to Chinatown that day."

"He did, didn't he?" The coil in his gut wound tighter. "You said you were careful that day."

"Absolutely, and then when I got close to Chinatown, it was such a big mess because of the parade I had to take a million detours. For each turn I made, I checked my rearview mirror. I even drove down a couple of little alleys—nothing."

"Elise, how many times did you see Ty since he came here?"

"Twice—once on the sidewalk in front of Courtney's place and just now." She combed her fingers through her hair. "Why are you asking? I certainly never told him anything about you or where you lived. I didn't even know where you lived until I followed you here tonight."

"You followed me here tonight." He dug his fingers in his hair.

"Um, yeah."

"There's only one way your stalker could've known about Ty."

"My stalker?"

"He saw him at Courtney's place—with you, with me."

Her head cranked back and forth. "No. That can't be. He doesn't know Courtney. He doesn't know where Courtney lives. How could he? He couldn't be that good, to be able to follow me around the city when I'm on the lookout for him. No way."

"He's not physically following you, Elise. He's tracking you." He barreled toward the coat closet by the front door and reached for the shelf for a flashlight.

"Tracking me? How?"

When he turned with the flashlight in his hand, he almost knocked her over.

Her eyes took up half her face as she grabbed his arm. "How is he tracking me?"

"I have a hunch." He threw open the front door with Elise hot on his heels. "Your car was parked in your garage when he broke in after the attack."

"My car… Yeah." She hooked her fingers in his belt loop. "Oh, God, you can't mean he put something on my car."

"That's exactly what I mean." He nudged her shoulder. "Pull it into the driveway next to mine so we can get it into the light."

Elise dashed to her car as Sean juggled the flashlight from hand to hand. If the killer had put some kind of tracking device on Elise's little hybrid, it would explain so much. It also meant he knew where she was staying and he knew she was here—right now.

His gaze scanned the street of empty cars parked at the curb. One car idled in the driveway, but that one belonged to his neighbor's teenage son who raced up and down the street daily.

Elise parked and exited her vehicle. "Where would he put something like that? Inside the car?"

"Most likely attached to the undercarriage of the chassis." He handed her the flashlight. "Hold this."

He dropped to his hands and knees, rolled onto his back and scooted under the front of the car. His nostrils flared at the smell of oil and gasoline, strong even for a hybrid. He thrust out his arm and wiggled his fingers. "Flashlight."

"Flashlight." Elise smacked it against his palm as if they were performing surgery.

He trailed the beam along the wheel wells and the undercarriage. He knew a bit about cars, and he didn't see anything amiss.

Maybe his instincts were off this time.

He shoved out from beneath the car and walked on his knees to the back. He ducked beneath the vehicle and swept the light back and forth. Rolling to one side, he aimed the beam at the wheel well.

"Bingo."

"What? You found something?" Elise's voice had risen to a frantic pitch.

He wrapped his fingers around the black box and yanked it from the metal, breaking the magnetic force. Gathering his legs beneath him, he rose to a crouch and cradled the device in the palm of his hand.

As Elise drew closer, he illuminated it with the flashlight.

"What is it?"

"It's a GPS tracking device."

She gasped and fell back on her hands. "It's been there since the night of the attack. He's been following me, tracking my every move. That's how he followed me to Chinatown. That's how he knew about my school. That's how he found out about Ty."

"It should've occurred to me sooner."

"That some killer would just happen to have a GPS tracking device handy?"

"He's a clever SOB."

"Sean!" She tugged on his arm, nearly toppling him over. "We have to warn Courtney. He knows where she lives, knows I'm staying there."

"Not anymore you're not. Give Courtney a call. You're staying here tonight, and I'll take you back to her place early tomorrow morning so you can get your things and get to school."

She jabbed her finger at the tracking device. "What are we going to do with this thing?"

"Oh, I have a plan. If the Alphabet Killer likes games, I've got a good one for him."

THE SOUND OF the alarm grated against her eardrums, and Elise sighed and snuggled closer to Sean's warm, smooth back.

She didn't want to move, didn't want to face the harsh world outside. But the alarm was insistent.

Sean growled and threw out an arm, his hand groping for the clock on the nightstand. With one well-aimed smack, he ended the sound that had intruded on Elise's sweet dreams.

She yawned and dug her chin into his shoulder. "You can't wake up to soothing music or wind chimes?"

"Those sounds would never wake me up. I have a hard enough time with that obnoxious noise blaring in my ear."

Elise squinted at the green numbers floating in the dark room. "Ugh, I haven't seen five o'clock a.m. since—since a maniac tried to kill me five days ago."

Sean swiveled around, twisting the covers in his legs, and pulled her against his chest. He kissed the top of her head. "He can't continue at this pace. You don't murder two people and dump their bodies in an alley without leaving a trail of clues."

She burrowed deeper into his arms and inhaled his scent. She wanted to bottle it and take it with her everywhere.

"Are you going to have to answer some questions about Ty today?"

"Of course, but I doubt my supervisors are going to believe I hired someone to mess up your ex-fiancé and then had my hit man tell him it was me."

He stroked her back and she almost purred. They hadn't made love last night after they'd discovered the GPS, but he'd held her all night long and that was almost as good.

"I want to be in on the questioning of Ty, so I hope they grant me that privilege since the guy accused me of chopping off his finger."

Her gut rolled. "I can't even think about that without feeling ill. Ty is going to be devastated when he wakes up and it all comes back to him."

"Ty should be thankful he's alive. I'm sure Katie Duncan wouldn't mind waking up about now missing one digit."

"You're right." She smoothed her hand down his arm, across his tattoo. "He has no idea how close he came to dying."

"We'd better get moving if we hope to collect your stuff from Courtney's and get you to school." He rolled away from her and planted his feet on the carpet. "She's checking into a hotel today, right? I think that's best right now."

"Yes. That girl has money to burn. She'll probably book a suite in some fancy hotel and live it up."

"When is she going back to pack up?"

"Well, since she spent the night with her new man, I think he's going to take her back."

"Have you met this new man of hers?"

"I met him briefly that night at the Speakeasy. He bought us a couple of drinks." She tumbled out of bed and shot him a quick glance. "You don't suspect him, do you?"

"Just covering all bases here."

"Derrick is African-American. I don't think he's the Alphabet Killer."

"Okay, okay. Does this Derrick look like he can handle himself in a fight?"

She hugged her sweater to her body. "Really? You think it's going to come to that? The killer probably doesn't even know who Courtney is."

"Can he?"

"He looks like he could've played football in college."

"Good." He pointed to the bathroom door. "I'm going to hit the shower first because I'll be quick about it."

She longed to hit the shower with him again, but there was no going back to that moment last night. But they'd have other moments—so he said.

An hour later, they stepped outside into the damp, misty air.

Sean tilted his head back. "June gloom is in full swing."

"Yeah, I pity all those tourists who come out here expecting a sunny California day."

"Spoken like a true San Franciscan native." He tossed the GPS device in the air and then clamped it back under her car.

"So what is your plan? You're just going to let him continue following me around?"

"You'll see. First stop, Courtney's condo."

Elise drove back into the city, and the tracker on her car made her feel exposed and vulnerable. She hated that. Only Sean's presence behind her made it bearable.

While Sean waited by the front door of Courtney's condo with his arms crossed, daring anyone to cross the threshold, Elise buzzed around the spare room and bathroom, tossing her stuff into her suitcase.

Joining Sean at the entrance, she took a last look around the immaculate downstairs. "If Courtney's homeowners' association was mad about the garlic, just wait until those fine folks discover she invited a killer to their complex."

Sean loaded her suitcase into the back of her car. "You follow me now. We're going to take a little detour. You have plenty of time to get to school, right?"

"Uh-huh. It's an easy day today. We're taking the kids over to the first-grade rooms to have a look around, and they get to wear their PJs to school and look at their favorite books all day."

"Wish I could wear my PJs to work and read my favorite books all day."

"I'd like to see that. What kind of PJs do you have, dinosaurs?"

He winked. "My PJs are my birthday suit, and you've already seen that."

"You're in enough trouble with the department. Don't

give them any more ammunition." Elise slid into her car and idled while Sean revved the engine of his Crown Vic.

She followed him across the city in the opposite direction of the Bay Bridge, hoping he didn't plan to take her too far afield.

Her cell buzzed and she answered and tapped the phone for the speaker, without checking the display. "Hello?"

"It's Courtney. Did you get your stuff?"

"I just picked it up. Aren't you the early bird?"

"I want to get home, pack a few suitcases and get the hell out of there. How long has this maniac been watching my place?"

"I'm so sorry, Courtney."

"I'm not blaming you. Hey, it gives me an excuse to get pampered at a hotel for a week or eight. When is your cop going to nail this guy?"

"Soon. Is Derrick going with you?"

"Oh, yeah. That's one silver lining. I get to play the little delicate flower in distress."

Elise snorted. "Yeah, that description fits you to a T."

"Derrick's digging it, so who am I to disappoint him?"

"I can't imagine you disappointing any man."

"Watch it. Don't believe everything you see on YouTube."

Elise laughed. "Take care. I'll touch base with you later. Are you working late?"

"Yes. New clients are running me ragged, but I can't complain. Business is good. One of the new guys said he chose me because of my name."

"Is he Asian?"

"No, but he had an Asian girlfriend, a hand model. He's probably projecting, but it gives us a lot to work with."

"Okay, you take care and let Derrick be the big, strong man."

"Mmm, he is."

Smiling, Elise ended the call and then gulped as Sean made a turn onto the road leading to the Golden Gate Bridge. Why the heck did he want to come here?

He pulled into the fog-shrouded parking lot and rolled into one of the many empty slots.

Elise parked beside him and jumped from the car as he was getting out of his.

"Are you crazy? What are we doing here?"

He put his finger to his lips and strode to her car. He ducked under her car and pulled the GPS from the wheel well. "Follow me and get that jacket out of your car."

Elise snagged a jacket from the backseat and shoved her arms in the sleeves.

They trudged up the path to the pedestrian gate on the bridge. Cars rumbled back and forth across the expanse on their morning commute. A few scattered pedestrians and cyclists dotted the walkway.

"Sean."

He turned toward her and zipped up her jacket to her chin. "Keep up."

They stepped onto the sidewalk on the east side of the bridge, the only side that allowed pedestrians.

Sean took a deep breath. "It's beautiful, isn't it? Even engulfed in fog, it's majestic, mysterious."

"I told you. It mesmerized me from the moment I saw it."

"We used to cross it a lot on foot. My younger brother Ryan used to look over the guardrail and insist he could do a pencil dive and just slice through the water."

She reached for his hand and laced her fingers with his.

Before reaching the midpoint, Sean stopped and faced the water. He plunged his hand in his pocket and pulled out the GPS. He stretched his arm back and flung the black box over the guardrail and into the bay. "Let that SOB track that."

A sharp breeze stirred up the mist, and the moisture caressed her face. “Why here, Sean? Why this spot?”

He gazed out toward Alcatraz, his face a mask. “Because this is where he did it. This is where my father jumped.”

Chapter Fifteen

Elise eyed the big clock on the wall as she read the last few lines of the story of Ferdinand the bull, who liked to smell flowers all day. What a life.

Ty was recuperating in the hospital and was demanding to see her. This was one of Ty's demands she was only too happy to oblige.

The bell rang while she and her students were dragging the beanbags and pillows back into the corners of the room. "Last day of school tomorrow. Bring your best smiles for the party and get ready for first grade."

She waved and smiled until her cheeks hurt, and then she packed up her bag.

Viola's husband stopped by, wedging his shoulder against the doorjamb. "You doing okay, Elise?"

"I'm fine. Just wrapping up."

"I heard about the two murders. The boys down in homicide getting any closer to nailing this guy?"

"I hope so." She turned off her classroom light and joined him at the door. "Are you looking forward to going to Alabama?"

He rolled his eyes. "Not at all. I'll walk you to your car since Vi's talking with a parent right now."

She tossed her bag in the backseat and hung on the door of her car. "Thanks for the escort."

"You bet. Take care and tell those boys in SFPD to call us in if they need any help."

"I'm sure they'd take that in the spirit it was meant."

He grinned as she slipped onto the driver's seat and shut the door.

She raced back across the bridge into the city. She'd see Ty alone, but Sean had promised to meet her at the hospital. He hadn't been in on the questioning of Ty, but he'd heard through certain channels that Ty had retracted his accusation against him.

At least his department didn't believe Sean was capable of that.

She pulled into the parking structure of the hospital—the same one where she'd met Sean less than a week ago, although it seemed like an eternity. How had they gotten so close so fast?

For some reason, the killer had targeted them both and that had given them some sort of shared purpose. Would that connection end when the killings did? She didn't want to be bound to Sean through some sick individual's obsession.

She joined a group in the elevator and rode up to the lobby of the hospital. From there she took another elevator to the fourth floor and checked in with the nurses' station.

"I'm here to see Ty Russell. Elise Duran."

The nurse at the desk tapped a few keys on the keyboard and nodded. "Four fifteen, down the hall to your right."

Elise thanked her and made her way down the antiseptic-smelling corridor, her running shoes squeaking on the shiny floor. When she reached Ty's room, she peered through the glass at him reclining on the hospital bed, watching TV.

She rapped one knuckle against the window, and his head jerked up. He beckoned to her with his right hand—the unbandaged one.

Lifting the door handle, she pushed through with her hip. "How are you, Ty? You look a lot better. Got your color back."

"I'm just great." He lifted his heavily bandaged left hand. "Except I'm missing my finger."

"I'm so sorry. That must've been horribly painful, but why in the world did you head to Sean—Detective Brody's house instead of the emergency room?"

"I don't know." He muted the TV. "I was in shock. I was in a rage."

"You couldn't possibly have believed that Detective Brody would send someone after you and that person would then reveal who hired him."

"I guess it's pretty stupid now that I think about it."

"Were you able to give the police a description?"

"Didn't the detective tell you? The man that attacked me was wearing a black ski mask over his face, and a bulky jacket. He was shorter than me and a lot heavier. If he hadn't ambushed me, I could've taken him."

"I feel terrible that you got all mixed up in this. You should've never come out here."

"Really, Elise? When your landlord, Oscar, called me and told me what had happened, how could I *not* come out?"

She sighed and wound a strand of hair around her finger. "Ty, I'm not your concern anymore."

"Are you worried about the finger? It's just my ring finger. I can't wear a wedding ring on the hand, but at least it's not my index finger or thumb."

"The finger—that means nothing, but I can't believe you're talking to me about wedding rings. If we were so great together, you never would've cheated. It's over between us, Ty."

"It's that cop."

"It is not that cop. How many times have I told you

this past year that I had moved on?" She patted his knee beneath the sheet. "You should, too. Give it a try with Gina. You must've seen something in her to risk our engagement."

His mouth dropped open. "Gina? She's a waitress at the Cozy Café."

She raised her eyes to the ceiling, remembering all over again why she'd had her doubts about him. "I can't help you there, Ty."

She snatched her hand back and rubbed it against her jeans. "I'm curious and you've probably already told the police, but how did you get Sean's address?"

"He gave it to me." Ty studied his bandaged hand. "The Alphabet Killer gave it to me."

A chill zigzagged down her spine. "Go home, Ty. Go back to Montana."

They chatted a bit more about home until Ty's pain meds kicked in and his eyelids began to droop and his words began to slur.

Elise tiptoed out of the room and practically ran into Sean coming around the corner at the nurses' station.

Grabbing her shoulders to steady her, he said, "I was hoping to run into you."

"And you did—literally."

"You look washed out, although it could just be the lighting. Are you okay? Did Ty give you a hard time?"

"Not really. He started the conversation still believing there was a chance that I'd go back to Montana with him, but I think he's getting the picture now."

"He's probably halfway in shock. That was a nasty business, and he was just in the wrong place at the wrong time."

"You know the killer gave him your address?"

"The detective questioning him told me."

"Do you think he knew your address before he tracked my car there?"

"Probably." He tapped her head. "Don't get it into this thick skull of yours that you led him to my place."

"Was there any evidence with the bodies?"

He cupped her elbow. "Let's get something to drink in the cafeteria. We can't talk here, and I'm not even supposed to be hanging around Ty's room. I'm off the case, remember?"

They took the elevator down to the lobby and crossed to the other side of the building to the hospital cafeteria. They both filled up sodas from a self-serve machine and snagged a table in the back of the noisy room filled with clattering plastic trays and hushed conversations.

"So, what do you know?"

Sean took a long sip from his straw. "Only what I got from Curtis. It's a lot different when you're not on the scene."

"I can't believe they're keeping you away. You know more about this case than anyone."

"If anything, they were justified in their actions today when Ray Lopez showed up and started wondering aloud why the lead detective wasn't at the crime scene."

"How did Lopez even know it was the work of the Alphabet Killer?"

"He didn't. Just fishing." He jiggled the ice in his cup and tilted it toward the soda machines. "I'm getting a refill. How about you?"

"Diet."

He returned with the cups topped off.

"Sean, was that cop last night right? Did the victims both have names that started with the letter C?"

"Yes. They were a married couple."

She bit down on her knuckle. "That's awful. Wh-where are their fingers?"

"I'm not discussing this with you, Elise. You don't need

to know the details, and don't get all in my face and tell me you have a right to know. I'm not falling for that."

"I'm not going to play that card." She folded her hands on the table in front of her. "But I would like to know what was in the note. That can't be too gory, can it?"

"The note." He plucked a napkin from the metal dispenser and lifted a pen from his pocket. He scribbled as he spoke. "Fifty-one plus fifty equals 187. Forty-two plus fifty-eight equals 187."

Elise cocked her head. "Makes no sense at all."

"He's just yanking our chain."

"Have you tried to decipher it yet?"

"Haven't given it a lot of thought. It's not my case, remember?"

"Even though he sent the note to you?"

"It's not like I can run around and investigate the case on my own. I'm not like my brother Judd."

"What does your brother Judd do?"

"He's a P.I., a private investigator. He follows a different drummer. He could never report to anyone. He's a rebel who distrusts authority."

"Where does he come in the line of Brody brothers?"

"He's my youngest brother."

"That makes sense. He probably remembers your father the least and has the most flimsy connection to him. Sounds like he might have grown up distrusting authority."

"Wow, are you picking up tips from Courtney or something?"

She stirred her ice with her straw. "Some things don't take a degree in psychology. They're just obvious."

"Well, you're probably right about Judd. He doesn't see what the big deal is. He can almost accept that his father was a serial killer and move on."

"But you can't."

"Never."

"He didn't know him like you did. How old was he when your father jumped?"

"He was six years old."

"A baby, like my kids."

"Yeah, he missed Dad and would cry himself to sleep when he was gone, but he didn't really understand what was going on."

"Reminds me a lot of my kids. So many of them come from broken homes or they never knew their fathers, and their moms are busy supporting the family. In many ways, it's just best if they move on, find another father figure."

"That's what Judd did. He's a carefree SOB. Wish I could be more like him."

She traced the grooves of his knuckles. "You were the oldest. You were his father figure, and you couldn't afford to be carefree."

"Not then, but maybe I should move on, too." He crossed an ankle over his knee. "Is Ty going home?"

"As soon as the hospital releases him. I think he's had enough of San Francisco."

"I'm sorry he got caught up in this." He turned his hand over and captured her fingers. "It's interesting that the killer has taken the index fingers of all his victims, but he chopped off Ty's ring finger. Do you think that has some significance?"

She tapped her cup. "Funny you should bring that up. Ty was talking about how he couldn't wear a wedding ring anymore. It's almost like the Alphabet Killer knew about our situation, almost like he was protecting me from Ty."

Sean slapped his palm against the table. "I'm glad you see that, too. That's exactly what I was thinking. He seems to have fixated on you, Elise."

She hunched her shoulders. "I don't want him fixated on me."

"Of course not, but in a way it makes me feel better. I

don't think he's going to hurt you. It's almost as if once you escaped from him, he developed some respect for you and is putting on a show just for you."

"Yuck. I wish he'd stop. I've had enough." She tapped the table in front of him. "Does the note mean he's going to kill again?"

"I don't see how he's going to keep up this pace. A killing takes a lot out of someone—emotionally, physically. He's already killed three people this week. Some serial killers go months between kills."

"He's going to screw up. I just know it. Attacking Ty like that was totally out of control."

"It feels like he's heading for some kind of climax."

"Sexual?"

"That's also something curious about this guy. So many serial killers rape their victims. The victims haven't shown any signs of molestation."

"Of course, that would just leave more evidence like DNA. He's very careful, isn't he?"

He sucked down the rest of his soda, slurping at the end. "Sorry. Do you want another?"

"I've had enough caffeine. I'm going to have a hard enough time getting to sleep tonight."

He grabbed her hand. "You're staying with me, right? That's decided."

"Courtney invited me to join her in her fabulous suite."

"Would you rather be with Courtney in her fabulous suite, or with me in my not-so-fabulous house?"

She ran her tongue along her bottom lip and stared deep into his dark eyes. "Your house was about the most fabulous place I've ever been—especially your shower."

"Such impure thoughts from a kindergarten teacher." He wiggled his eyebrows up and down. "Do you need to go back to your place or Courtney's to get anything?"

"Probably not a bad idea to drop by my place even

though I packed enough the first time around to get me through the week."

"You know—" he ran his knuckles down her forearm "—it might not be a bad idea for you to get out of the city when school's over. Did you have any plans before all this broke?"

"I was actually just going to take a week or so and drive down the coast—you know, through Monterey, Big Sur and maybe as far south as Hearst Castle. I've never been to any of those places."

"That's a great drive. You'll love it. Can you do that sooner rather than later?"

"Are you trying to get rid of me?"

"Trying to keep you safe."

She hunched forward. "Sean, tell me you're going to catch this guy."

"Me?" He jabbed his chest with his thumb. "I'm not allowed to catch him. I'll be picking up other cases and leaving the Alphabet Killer to the task force—the task force I'm not on."

"That's crazy."

Sean's eyebrows collided over his nose. "Fifty-one fifty."

"Huh?"

"The call for picking up someone mentally unstable—fifty-one fifty."

"Okay, if you say so."

He shoved the napkin in front of her. "Fifty-one fifty. It's in the note."

"Is he telling us he's crazy? We already know that." She folded up one edge of the napkin as she studied the other numbers. "Could this be a coordinate again?"

"I don't know, Elise. Could be anything and could be a total red herring like the coordinates for the Golden Gate Bridge."

She tapped some ice from the cup into her mouth. "I wonder what he thought when he tracked my GPS right into the bay."

"I hope he realized two can play stupid mind games." He rolled up the napkin and stuffed it in his pocket. "He loves those mind games."

"And fingers."

"Is Ty going to be okay?"

"He'll get over it. Like you said, I think he's beginning to realize he's lucky to be alive."

"And he's beginning to realize it's over between the two of you? Is it over?"

"Of course. Did you think I'd feel so much sympathy for his finger I'd go back to him?"

"I think he was hoping you would."

"I set him straight."

Sean pushed back from the table. "Unless you want to eat hospital cafeteria food, let's get going."

"I'm in the parking structure below."

"Not a great idea, Elise."

"We got rid of the GPS. He's not tracking my movements anymore."

"We don't know what he's up to." He patted his pocket with the napkin. "He's obviously on the hunt for a new victim."

"Does the task force have any idea how he finds his victims?" She dropped her cup in the trash. "Any idea how he found me?"

"We…they're looking into everything, Elise." He glanced up and pointed. "That guy can tell you more than I can now."

Detective Curtis was barreling into the cafeteria and didn't notice them until Sean raised his hand.

Curtis's eyebrows jumped. "You didn't drop in on the vic, did you?"

Sean placed his hand on her arm. “She did. Don’t worry—I stayed well away.”

“Was Ty able to tell you anything, Detective Curtis?”

“You can call me John.” He skimmed the top of his short hair with the palm of his hand. “He couldn’t tell us much. Guy came at him out of nowhere.”

“Are you heading up the task force now?” Elise shifted from one foot to the other, brushing Sean’s arm. He seemed to be taking his removal from the task force well, but his body still seemed tight and tense.

Curtis shot an apologetic look at Sean. “Yeah, the captain has me running the show. Hey, did you see Jacoby wandering around? I thought he was coming down to get prints on the vic. Sorry, Ty.”

“I didn’t. Why, did you find a finger?”

“Not yet. I hope it doesn’t wind up in the mail to you.”

“What is this guy’s obsession with fingers, anyway?” Elise shoved her hands in her pockets.

Sean snorted. “Who knows? Maybe he got sick of people pointing fingers at him and decided to lop them off.”

“It’s sick and weird.”

“And right now, it’s Curtis’s problem.” Sean grabbed her hand. “Let’s get the rest of your stuff and move it to my place.”

Curtis coughed. “Elise is staying with you now?”

“I told you, her friend’s place was compromised. Her friend’s in a hotel, and I think Elise would be safer with me.”

“You know there’s going to be hell to pay when the captain figures out you tossed that GPS device into the bay?”

“Had to do it. Do you think we would’ve gotten anything from it? The Alphabet Killer is too careful with his fingerprints, and if he’s that careful with his prints he probably knows to file off the serial number on any device he uses.”

“You’re right, Brody. That’s why you should be heading up this case.”

Sean smacked him on the back. “You’ll do fine, Curtis, but in the meantime Elise is coming home with me, and you can tell the captain that, too.”

“The captain doesn’t have to know everything.” He winked and then rubbed his hands on his way to the hot-food counter.

Elise turned to Sean in the elevator and said, “I can’t figure out if John is happy he’s got the task force or upset.”

“Probably a little of both. It’s always good for your career to lead a task force, but he’s worked in my shadow for a long time.”

“Do you think he resents that?”

“John?” Sean stabbed at the elevator button for the parking garage a few more times. “He’s too good-natured for that.”

“Still, I get the impression that you’re the superstar detective in the homicide department.”

“I’ve solved a few big cases, but it’s all a team effort. I couldn’t do my job without all the support people.”

“With all the little people?”

The elevator doors trundled open on the second floor of the parking garage, and Sean wedged his shoulder against one side of the opening to hold the door open for her.

“Is that how it sounded to you?”

“Not at all. You sounded very modest, but I just wonder if everyone sees it that way.”

“Curtis knows the score. He’s good at some things and I’m good at other things.”

She clicked her remote. “Where are you parked?”

“Out front. Give me a ride to my car and I’ll follow you back to your place.”

“My place. I don’t even know where that is anymore.”

When they'd collected her things and returned to Sean's place, he stepped over the brownish spot on his carpet where Ty had collapsed. "I don't think that stain will ever come out. I'll have to get the carpet replaced or forever be reminded of Ty accusing me of hiring someone to attack him before passing out on my floor."

"Ty was crazy with shock and confusion. Obviously the guy planted that in his head."

"You know that accusation made my blood boil even though I knew there was no chance that you or anyone else would believe it. I'd fight to the bitter end to clear my name if someone unjustly accused me of a crime." He shoved his hands in his pockets. "I just can't understand why my father didn't do the same."

"You just can't know what was going through his head, Sean."

Elise dropped one of her bags in the corner next to the only plant in the room, making its leaves wave.

Sean snapped out of his reverie. "Hey, watch it. That plant's barely alive as it is."

She flicked her fingers at it as if to dismiss it. "Looks like it's doing as well as the plants in my classroom. Just one more day of school."

"And then you're going to take that trip down the coast?"

"Maybe." She tossed her hair over her shoulder. "Do you think he'll stop sending you messages when he knows you're off his case?"

"You haven't been watching Ray Lopez. I think everyone in the city knows I'm off the case. He's not going to care about that."

"I guess not, since he left you a message with the bodies last night."

"Exactly."

"Fifty-one plus fifty. Fifty-one fifty."

"Uh-huh."

"Forty-two plus fifty-eight. That can't be a date. He's not going to commit a murder on April second and tell us about it today."

"Tell *us?*"

"You know what I mean." She reached for her purse. "That's my phone. It's Courtney." She picked up the call. "Hey, did you get checked in?"

"It's like a minivacation. You can join me if you like."

"I'm good where I am." Her gaze wandered to Sean, checking the messages on his phone.

"I'll bet you are."

"Thanks so much for letting me stay with you. I'm sorry I led a killer to your doorstep."

"How were you supposed to know the creep had bugged your car? Are you going to stay there with Detective Tall, Dark and Handsome until this guy is caught, or what?"

"I'm thinking of taking my vacation a little early."

Without looking up from his phone, Sean flashed her a thumbs-up.

Courtney concurred. "I think that's a great idea. Oscar should be home next week and I think that he'll be around all summer, not that he would be much help in an emergency, but at least you won't be coming home to an empty house."

"Maybe it'll be safe by then."

"Oops. Hold on a minute. The restaurant where I just ordered my dinner is calling me. They forgot to take my address." The phone beeped on the other end and then Courtney came back on the line. "Four twenty-five, eighth floor."

"What?"

"Oh, sorry. Wrong line."

"You sound busy."

Courtney huffed out a breath. “It’s that needy new client. I’m seeing him after hours again.”

“Well, you go figure out his craziness. I’ll talk to you later.”

She ended the call and pointed her phone at Sean. “Anything new?”

“I called for the autopsy report on Dr. Patrick.”

“And?”

“Preliminary report suggests heart attack.”

“Then maybe that’s all it was—a heart attack and bad timing.”

“A heart attack and an incredible coincidence.” He stretched and perched on the edge of a bar stool. “Is Courtney working late tonight?”

“Yes, her demanding new client.”

“That’s a whole lotta crazy I couldn’t handle.”

“And that’s from someone who gets a package with a finger in it.”

“Come here.” He crooked his finger at her.

She eased out of the chair and sauntered toward him, his dark eyes drawing her like a magnet.

He drew her between his open legs and pinned her. “I’m glad you’re here. I’m glad you’re safe.”

“I don’t know what I would’ve done without you, Sean.” She rested her hands on his thighs and leaned in to kiss his lips.

His legs tightened around her thighs. “Let’s go out and get something to eat. It’s getting late, and we both have to work tomorrow.”

Nodding, she slipped away from his clinch, missing her opportunity to ask him about their future. She didn’t want to push him into anything. Right now they needed each other, but when that need ended, what did they have?

“You okay?” He chucked her under the chin.

“Greek.”

"What?"

"I want to try that Greek restaurant, if that's okay with you and if it's still open this late."

"Greek it is. I think they stay open until eleven for dinner."

An hour later they were sitting at a corner table in a noisy establishment in North Beach.

"I can't believe it's so crowded at this time of night—and on a Wednesday." Elise leaned across the table. "Are they going to start breaking plates?"

"Do you want them to?"

She scooped more tapenade onto her plate. "That's okay."

Sean checked his phone for about the third time since they sat down to dinner.

"Are you expecting a call or a message? Something about Dr. Patrick?"

"I sent my brother—the FBI agent—a text about Dr. Patrick."

"So, let me get this straight. You're a homicide detective, you have one brother who's a P.I. and another who's FBI?"

"That's right."

"What's the fourth one?"

"Actually Ryan is the third one, and he's the police chief of Crestview."

"I guess the Brody blood really does run blue. Is there something the FBI agent can do in his position to get more information?"

"Not sure, but I'm asking."

She felt in her purse for her own phone. "Courtney was going to check in with me when she finished with her client."

She checked the display, but Courtney hadn't called or texted.

"Did she call? She's more than welcome to join us for dinner. We haven't gotten to the main course yet, and her office is close by, isn't it?"

"I'll invite her if she ever finishes up with this client. She hasn't called yet."

"She sure goes all out for her patients, doesn't she?"

"She comes across as a party girl, but she's really very serious about her work and very caring. And since she's a therapist, she calls them clients instead of patients."

"She can't prescribe medication, but I'm sure she has some clients that need it, right?"

"She refers them to a doctor she works with. She's had a few certifiably crazy clients, and she ended up transferring them to a psychiatrist she knows."

"Must be hard to deal with the really crazy ones."

"I don't think *crazy* is the term the professionals use." She bit into her cracker and dabbed her mouth with a napkin.

"Well, that's the term cops use." Sean drew his brows over his nose. "You did say Courtney's office was nearby, right?"

"Yeah, the address is forty-two something or four, two, something on Market."

Sean balanced his fork on the edge of his plate. "What floor is she on?"

His voice was so low it barely cut through the din, but the urgency behind the words had her looking up from her plate sharply.

"Floor? I don't remember." She gave up trying to stab the olive with her fork and pinched it between her fingers instead. "Why are you asking? Are you suggesting we bring the food to her?"

"No, I..."

She snapped her fingers. "Wait. She was getting food delivered to her office, and she thought I was the delivery guy and she rattled off her address and floor number. It was four, two something and the eighth floor, but I don't think she needs..." She trailed off, her gut twisting at Sean's tight face. "What is it?"

"The message, Elise. The message from the Alphabet Killer. Fifty-one plus fifty equal 187. Forty-two plus fifty-eight equal 187."

She blinked and gulped some water to wash down the sour taste of fear. "I don't get it."

"We already guessed that the fifty-one, fifty might mean crazy, as in the type of clients Courtney might see. If her address is four, two, five on the eighth floor—forty-two plus fifty-eight—we have a problem."

She'd already shoved back from the table. "You mean Courtney has a problem. She's in danger."

Sean pulled out his wallet and dropped several twenties on the table. "I'm going to call this in, but let's head over there now."

Elise kept stabbing at the redial button on the way out of the restaurant, but the call rolled over to Courtney's voice mail every time. When they hit the sidewalk, Elise took a deep breath after Courtney's recorded greeting. "Courtney, it's Elise. I don't want to freak you out or anything, but once you're done with your client, don't see anyone else and just wait in your office with the door locked. Sean and I are heading over there right now. It's about ten-thirty. Call me as soon as you get this if we don't see you first."

By the time they reached Sean's car, Elise's breath was coming out in short spurts.

Sean buckled his seat belt and chucked his phone against the dashboard. "They won't come. The lieutenant on duty thinks it's a wild-goose chase and is refusing to send a patrol car."

"What about John?"

"He's off duty. I tried him at home, but he's not there or he's not picking up."

"Hurry, Sean. It's not that far. Maybe she's still with a client. I told her to stay in her office and lock the door."

Sean's tires squealed as he shot into the street, horns honking in his wake.

"Elise, did Courtney ever tell you anything about this new client of hers, the one who was so demanding?"

She clamped down on her bouncing knees. "No. Why are you asking me that?"

But she knew why. The same thought had been niggling at her brain since Sean started putting together the puzzle of the note.

"She started seeing that guy right after you were attacked, right after you moved in with her."

Elise doubled over, sinking her face in her hands. "He found her because of me."

"Maybe. This is all just supposition right now."

She shot up, pain pounding behind her eyes. "Courtney did mention something about him today."

"Description, name?"

"She wouldn't break that confidentiality." She stared unseeing out the car window. "She told me how he picked her out."

"How?"

"Her name." She dug her fingernails into Sean's thigh. "He chose her because he liked her name, Sean. Courtney Chu. Two Cs. He's still on the Cs."

With this last bit of news, Sean whipped around the next corner and tossed his phone at her. "Try calling Curtis again. Leave him a message. Tell him we're on our way to Courtney's and give him the address again."

Elise followed his instructions and by the time she ended the call, Sean had pulled up in front of Courtney's office building.

Elise scrambled out of the car before it came to a complete stop. She grabbed on to the two long silver handles of the glass doors and yanked. They didn't budge. She pressed her face against the glass, her eyes searching the lobby.

Sean joined her and picked up the phone to the right of the doors. "This is SFPD Homicide Detective Sean Brody. We're trying to get into the building to see Courtney Chu on the eighth floor."

He listened for a minute and then replaced the receiver. "That was security. They're sending someone down."

Elise kept hold of the door handles as if that could make them arrive sooner. "It's dark, it's locked up. Maybe Courtney left already. Maybe she's out with Derrick. It's so late."

"Here's the security guard." Sean opened his ID and pressed his badge against the glass.

The doors clicked, and the security guard swung one open. "Is there a problem?"

"We're here to check on Courtney Chu, eighth floor. Have you seen her? Has she left for the night?"

"I know Ms. Chu. She had some food delivered a while back, but I haven't seen her since."

"Did anyone come to the office to see her? Anyone you had to let in?"

"No, sir. We lock the doors at ten o'clock. If she had a client before then, I wouldn't have opened the door for him or her."

"Okay, thanks. We still want to check on her."

"Sure thing." He swung the door open wide and they stepped into the building. "From this point, you can go on up to the eighth floor."

"Can you come with us in case we need to get into Ms. Chu's office?"

"I have my rounds, but—" he pulled a key from his keychain "—this is the master and it'll get you in."

"Thanks." Sean took the key and pounded the button for the elevator. "One more thing."

The security guard stopped at the door to the right of the elevators with his hand on the doorknob. "Yes?"

"Has anything unusual happened tonight? Anything out of the ordinary?"

The guard cocked his head. "As a matter of fact, yes. An emergency buzzer sounded for one of the side doors about an hour ago."

Elise swallowed and curled her hand around Sean's arm. "What does that mean?"

"Means someone left the building by way of an emergency exit. Who knows? Maybe it was Ms. Chu."

"H-has she ever done that before?"

The security guard shook his finger. "That Ms. Chu likes to break the rules."

As they rode up to the eighth floor, Elise said, "Maybe that's it. Maybe Courtney's not even here."

"Maybe."

The doors opened, and Elise tugged on Sean's sleeve to steer him to the right. The silence enveloped them, and Elise held her breath. When they got to the door of Courtney's office, Elise let out a breath on a whispered prayer. "Please, God, let her be safe."

Sean tried the door handle first. Then he pulled out the key the security guard had given him and shoved it into the lock. He turned the lock and pushed the door at the same time, staggering into the small waiting room.

Elise had been in here once before and it looked the same—undisturbed. Courtney had fanned out the latest magazines on one low table and had stacked others in a holder on the wall. Two fake plants bobbed in the corners, and someone had left an indentation in one of the leather love seats.

The needy client who liked Courtney's name?

Elise marched toward the door to Courtney's inner sanctum, but Sean put out a steadying hand.

"Wait."

He drew his gun from his holster and crept toward the same door. Shoving Elise behind him, he eased open the door.

More silence.

Elise's nostrils flared and the blood thrummed in her eardrums.

Sean aimed his gun at the three closed doors off the hallway and whispered, "Which one is her office?"

The whisper sent a chill up her spine, but she shook off her fear and pointed to the first door on the left.

"Stay back."

Sean twisted the handle of the door and inched it open. He'd stepped into the office, but Elise was no longer watching him.

A slight movement on the floor to her right caught her eye. Her gaze darted to the tile in front of what she knew was the bathroom floor.

A trickle of dark liquid meandered from the crack beneath the door. As if in a trance, Elise stepped over it to push open the bathroom door. The door swung freely and then stopped.

She heard Sean's voice coming from the office, words she couldn't comprehend, words coming at her in a fog.

She opened her mouth and managed a small sigh. She ran her tongue along her teeth and tried again.

This time she managed a scream, a scream so loud it echoed and bounced off the walls of the small bathroom where Courtney's lifeless form couldn't hear her at all.

Chapter Sixteen

Sean shot a worried glance at Elise, slumped in the leather love seat in the waiting room, her eyes glassy, a grayish pallor to her cheeks.

Curtis was yammering at him. "You figured out the next victim was Courtney Chu from that cryptic note?"

Jacoby slapped Curtis on the back. "Brody's the best. Get used to it, Curtis."

"So you got some prints this time?"

Jacoby smiled and patted his bag. "If he was posing as a client and he'd been here before, maybe we'll get lucky."

Sean swung around on Melvin, the security guard. "Did you get the video from the cameras?"

"We're collecting that for you now, Detective Brody."

"But you didn't notice the guy coming in tonight?"

"Nope. The only one I saw was the delivery boy from the restaurant." He pointed at Curtis. "And I gave Detective Curtis the name of the restaurant."

Curtis held up his hand. "I'm on it. We're going to bring the kid in for questioning."

"The killer has to be on camera. I'm hoping we can get a good look at him on those videos."

Curtis lowered his voice and moved closer to Sean. "Sorry I wasn't available when you called, and there's going to be hell to pay for Healy for refusing backup."

"I don't know if it would've helped. Judging by the—" he slid a glance at Elise, who was sipping some water "—condition of the body, I think we were too late anyway."

The coroner had arrived and Sean slipped away from the crush of people and crouched in front of Elise, taking her hands.

"How are you doing?"

She raised her blue eyes, flooded with tears. "It's my fault. I brought him into her life."

He squeezed her hands. "It's his fault, Elise. His and no one else's."

"She was so full of life. I can't even imagine her silent forever." She pressed a hand to her forehead. "Has anyone notified her brother? Has anyone told Oscar yet?"

"They're working on that."

A tear crested on her lower lid and rolled down her cheek. "He screwed up, didn't he? Dan Jacoby told me he got a lot of prints. There has to be video of him coming in and out of the building as a client of Courtney's. He can't have come and gone through the emergency door every time he saw her."

"We'll get him. I promise you that. There will be justice for Courtney and the other three victims, too. Justice for you."

She dashed the tear from her cheek with the back of her hand. "How am I going to make it to the last day of school tomorrow? It's already past one-thirty."

"Take the day off. Everyone will understand."

"But the kids."

"You can see them next year when they're first-graders. I know you're a wonderful teacher, but they'll be so excited for the last day of school they won't be sad for long that you're not there."

"Maybe. I feel so awful. I don't even know if I can get up from this love seat."

"Sean!"

He twisted his head around and answered Curtis. "What is it?"

"Lieutenant Healy wants you down at the station—now."

"Are you kidding me? Don't tell me he's mad because I found the Alphabet Killer's victim."

"He's mad about a lot of things. I suggest you head down there."

Sean rose to his feet and brought Elise with him, tucked against his side. "Technically, I was on a date."

Curtis cleared his throat. "Technically, you were on a date with a witness, which is another one of his points of contention."

"I'm not leaving Elise stranded, and I don't want her going back to my place alone."

"Your place?" Curtis rolled his eyes. "Yeah, the LT doesn't even know about that, but he could add it to his list when he chews you out."

Elise pressed her shoulder against Sean's. "It's okay. There are a million cops here, and my guess is they'll be here for a few more hours. I can just stay here and wait for you."

Sean glanced at the coroner's stretcher in the hallway. "I don't want you hanging out here, Elise. You're exhausted."

"I'll tell you what." Curtis smiled at Elise. "You go have your confab with the lieutenant, and I'll take Elise out for coffee to wait for you or back to my place, or we can even go back to your place."

"Hot chocolate."

"Huh?"

"Elise likes hot chocolate with whipped cream." He hugged her close. "Is that okay with you?"

"Yes, of course. I don't want you to get into any more

trouble because of me." She sniffled. "I don't want to be the cause of any more trouble for anyone."

Sean gave her a quick kiss and didn't care who saw. "Hang in there, kid. I'll be with you as soon as I can."

She bobbed her head once and sank back down to the love seat.

"Take care of her, Curtis." Sean glanced over his shoulder at Elise one more time before leaving the crime scene.

When he got to the station, it looked like one o'clock in the afternoon instead of one o'clock in the morning. And Lieutenant Healy was presiding over all the controlled chaos with a tight rein.

When he saw Sean, he barked, "Brody. In here now."

Sean sat tight-lipped as the lieutenant dressed him down for consorting with a witness, for conducting an investigation on his own and even for continuing to thrust himself into this case when he'd been removed from it.

At the end of the tirade, he praised Sean for his good detective work and was personally inviting him back on the case.

"I'll deal with the captain tomorrow. He can't really believe you don't have something important to contribute, but—" he held up one crooked finger "—Curtis will still be lead. And if you have a problem…"

"No problem with that, sir."

"Good. Now let's head over to the situation room. The security office at the victim's building turned over the tapes. We have the victim's phone and appointment book, so we're going to try to match up some appointment times with the videos."

"I'm in."

He and the lieutenant and one of the junior detectives hunched over the laptop and fast-forwarded through people walking in and out of Courtney's building.

Sean tossed down his pencil in frustration. "There are a

lot of offices in that building and a lot of foot traffic. Elise Duran told me there were a few nights this week where the victim saw this new client later in the day. Let's concentrate on the video for those times when there aren't so many people."

When the videos were loaded, Sean peered at the grainy images on the laptop monitor. They stopped the video and captured and printed pictures of every man who came through the door.

When he had a stack, he said, "I'm going to run these by Elise so she can see if any of these guys look familiar."

He studied in particular a stocky man with a cap pulled low over his face, which he kept turned away from the camera. He could even be wearing a gray jacket, like the man who attacked Elise.

Rubbing his eyes, Sean checked his watch. He'd been here for almost two hours. He wanted, no, he needed to see Elise.

He grabbed the printouts and cruised down the hallway to the lab. Lieutenant Healy had the techs hopping in here, too.

Sean waved the papers in his hand. "I need a few of these blown up. Do we have anything on the fingerprints from the office yet?"

Kwan looked up from his computer. "Fingerprints? We don't have no stinkin' fingerprints yet."

"Jacoby hasn't been back here with his treasures yet? I thought he'd be gleefully running prints about now."

"Jacoby does love him some fingerprints, but he hasn't come back from the crime scene."

"Are they still out there?"

"Oh, yeah."

Sean furrowed his brow and smacked the printouts down on the counter. "Okay, can someone work on these?

I'm going to check in with the LT, and then I'm outta here. Call me if something comes up."

Sean returned to his desk to file some notes and then started for the lieutenant's office. His heart stuttered when he saw Curtis through the glass talking to Healy.

Had he brought Elise here?

He stalked to the office and pushed open the door. "Where's Elise? Did you bring her down here?"

Curtis turned and leaned against the lieutenant's desk. "No, I had more work to do at the crime scene and then the lieutenant called me back here."

"Where is she? You didn't leave her alone, did you?"

"Relax, loverboy." Curtis shifted a quick glance at Healy and grimaced. "I left her with Jacoby. He said he'd take her back to your place and stick around until you got there."

Jacoby. The adrenaline continued to course through Sean's body and he charged out of the lieutenant's office and back to the lab.

"Have you singled out those stills from the video yet?" Sean had punched in Elise's cell phone number, but it had tripped over to voice mail.

Kwan's mouth dropped open. "Dude, you just dropped off the printouts. We haven't had time to match them on the video yet."

Sean pulled out a chair at one of the computers and opened the portions of the video they'd marked. He scanned through and stopped at the image of the man in the baseball cap. "Kwan, come here."

Kwan hovered over his shoulder. "What?"

Jabbing his finger at the screen, Sean asked, "Doesn't this look like Jacoby to you?"

Adjusting his glasses, Kwan leaned in. "Could be, same shape, but Jacoby's built rock solid. This guy looks a little heavyset to me."

"That could be the jacket, right? A guy with big muscles might look heavy in a puffy jacket."

"Sure, but what are you saying? Jacoby was in that building? I mean, he could've been—dentists, lawyers, hell, even steroid docs. So what?"

"Fingers. Fingerprints."

"What the hell, Brody?"

"How come there hasn't been one set of prints to come out of any of these murders? Not even a partial."

"The Alphabet Killer wears gloves. He's careful."

"He knows police procedures."

"Jacoby's weird, but he ain't that weird."

Sean's head jerked to the side. "What do you mean by *weird?*"

"I don't know." Kwan wiped his mouth with the back of his hand. "With the ladies. He trolls those online dating forums but can never get up the guts to make a move."

The blood was roaring in Sean's ears now. He stormed out of the lab and interrupted Curtis and Healy. "Where's Jacoby?"

Curtis smirked. "Why? Do you think he's moving in on your woman?"

Sean smacked his hand against the doorjamb. "This isn't a joke, John. I think Jacoby might be our killer."

Both men stared at him, but they weren't laughing.

"That's crazy, Sean."

"Brody, unless you have some hard evidence, you'd better put a cork in it."

"Here." Sean drilled his fist into his gut. "I feel it here."

"You're a good enough detective to know that's not good enough." Healy had sat back down in dismissal.

"Fingers, the guy loves his fingerprints." Curtis scratched the stubble on his chin. "What do you need, Sean?"

Healy glared at them from beneath his eyebrows. "You two can take this outside my office."

When the door shut behind them, Curtis turned to Sean. "What do you need me to do?"

"Look at his schedule, John. See where he's been at the time of the murders. Review that video for me. One of the guys walking in that building looks like Jacoby." He grabbed his shoulders. "Did he ask to watch over Elise?"

Curtis squeezed his eyes closed. "Sort of. Let's just say he was eager to take over the job when I got called away."

"Damn. Where'd they go? What kind of car does he have?"

"We can look up his car here. He told me he was taking her to that twenty-four-hour coffee shop near the park."

"Thanks for your help, John. I know you can get in trouble for this if it's all in my head."

"I'll bet on you every time, Brody."

Sean yelled over his shoulder as he took off toward the elevators, "Keep me posted."

When he got to his car, he punched in Elise's phone number again. This time when he got her voice mail, he left her a message. "Elise, where are you? Call me as soon as you get this message and don't trust Jacoby. If you're with him, make some excuse to get away and then—get away. Run away from him as fast as you can."

He cranked on his engine and swung out of the parking garage. His phone buzzed in the cup holder, where he'd tossed it, signaling a message, and he grabbed it. He blew out a breath when he saw Elise's name on the display.

He balanced the phone on the steering wheel to click on the message. Then he slammed on his brakes, sending his car into a fishtail as he read the message: Elise is busy. Thirty-seven plus forty-nine plus 122 plus twenty-eight equal 187.

The coordinates for the Golden Gate Bridge.

ELISE COUGHED AND gagged as Jacoby dragged her from the trunk of his car—a different car than the one he'd had at their first meeting.

He shoved her in front of him, prodding her back with

the barrel of his .45. "No running away this time, Elise. Guns are not my weapon of choice—too much evidence in the form of ballistics and blood spatter. You see, I'm just as good a detective as Brody."

She licked her dry lips. "Where's your phony English accent?"

"The same place as my phony cast, beat-up car and fake beard." He nestled close to her side and she gagged on his cologne. "You have to admit that was a pretty good disguise. Nothing even registered for you when I came to your house not twelve hours later. Of course, I didn't think it would since you wouldn't expect a homicide field tech to be a killer, would you?"

"Something about you rubbed me the wrong way from the beginning."

"Yeah, yeah. That's what they all say. Keep walking."

"Where are we going?" But she didn't have to ask. Even though he'd parked his car in the gravel parking lot on the other side of the tourist center, the Golden Gate Bridge soared above them, just peeking from the early morning fog that swirled around it.

He clicked his tongue. "Just trying to make small talk, Elise? You know where we're going."

"W-we can't go onto the bridge. It's closed to pedestrians at this time of night."

"It's actually morning, but who's counting?" Smiling, he showed her a black, square device in his hand. "I'm sure I mentioned that I'm a cyclist, and we get special privileges for the bridge."

Elise shivered but plodded on ahead of Jacoby. Would he force her to jump? He'd have to shoot her first. She'd never jump off that bridge. Maybe he just planned to slice her up as he did the others. As he did Courtney.

She hugged herself. She should've never gone with Jacoby when John had to leave. She could've just stayed at the crime scene or waited with security at the building until Sean came back for her.

"Sean's going to know it's you. Why else would you take off with me?"

"Well—" his feet crunched on the gravel behind her "—I thought of that and figured I could just tell him I took you back to his place and had to leave myself. I'd be beating myself up about leaving you alone, but you'd still be dead."

"He'll never believe you. You're leaving too many clues, too much evidence."

"Ah, evidence. I'm quite good at covering up, but I have other plans for Detective Sean Brody."

Elise's heart jumped. "You're not going to hurt him?"

"What is it about all that dark brooding masculinity that drives women wild? I believe you'd die for him. Would you, Elise? Would you die for him?"

"Shut up."

"You must get that level of maturity from your kindergartners, like that little Eli."

She whipped around on him. "What do you know about Eli?"

"Enough." He shoved her and she tripped. "Now get moving."

Her teeth began to chatter as the chill seeped into her bones. Just like that other night. Would she wind up in the bay again?

He clicked his remote control device, which unlocked the security gate to the pedestrian walkway. He pushed it open and left it ajar.

"Won't the cyclists be suspicious about an open gate?"

"Happens more than you think. Besides, I'm expecting company."

Again, her heart lurched in her chest just as her feet hit the pavement of the walkway. Would any cyclists be crossing at this time of morning? It had to be getting close to three o'clock. The walkway opened at five to pedestrians.

But something told her they wouldn't be here at five.

"Stop."

She slowed her steps and grabbed a lamppost. "What are we doing?"

"Waiting. Have you ever wondered how it would feel to jump, Elise? Four seconds. They say it takes four seconds to fall before you hit the water. That's a long time to change your mind."

"People must be desperate, lonely."

"Or guilty." His gun hand wavered. "I get lonely sometimes. Does it fascinate you, Elise? This bridge? It fascinates me. Always has, and I grew up here."

"It's beautiful. Maybe that's why they choose to have their last moments here."

He snorted. "You know nothing of depression or desperation. The last thing on your mind is beauty."

"Why don't you just turn yourself in, Dan?"

"You remember my name? Seems like you only had eyes for Brody."

"Of course I remember your name, Dan. C-Courtney liked you, too. She told me about her new client. She liked you."

"Courtney is beautiful."

"She would've helped you, Dan."

"She tried. She wanted to."

His aim had slipped, and she tensed her muscles. Could she tackle his legs?

"Elise!"

She jerked her head up to see Sean jogging toward them on the pedestrian path. How had he found them?

The smile spreading across Jacoby's face told that story.

"Perfect." Jacoby grabbed Elise's arm and dragged her closer, the gun leveled at her head. "Stop where you are,

Brody. This time I was telling the truth about the coordinates."

Sean's chest heaved and every breath pained him. What did this psycho plan to do with Elise? "It's over, Jacoby. When I saw your car in the parking lot, I called it in. How did you expect to get away with this?"

"Does this spot look familiar to you, Brody? Do you know this spot on the bridge? Have you been here before?"

"It's where my father jumped. It's where they found his things."

Elise sobbed, her face a pale oval in the mist.

"Exactly. And now you're going to do the same thing."

"No!" The fog swallowed Elise's scream.

"You're going to murder the lovely Elise, and then the Alphabet Killer is going to jump, just like his father the Phone Book Killer did."

Sean ground his teeth. "My father was not a killer."

"That's funny. My mother never believed he did it, either."

"What?"

"We lived in the city then. It was the Phone Book Killer who got me interested in police work, in homicide. I always thought he did it, but my mother claimed nobody that handsome could be a killer." He shrugged his massive shoulders. "You Brodys live charmed lives."

"Yeah, really charmed."

He yanked Elise's hair. "Do you want mine instead? My father was a petty thief and pimp, in and out of jail. Your father even arrested him once for domestic battery. How about that?"

"You have a good life, Jacoby. You're respected in your field."

"*My* field isn't *your* field. I wanted to be a police officer. I wanted to be a homicide detective." He shoved Elise against the guardrail. "I didn't pass the background. Now, how is it I couldn't pass the background with my father but you could with yours?"

"Maybe it was your psych eval, Jacoby. How much do you think you can hide?"

"How much can you?"

"I never tried to hide anything. Is that what this is all about? You're jealous of my wonderful career and life, so you went on a killing rampage."

Jacoby slapped Elise across the face, and Sean clenched his fists and took a step forward.

"Not really, Brody. I just like hurting people. I guess I am like my old man, and you're going to be just like yours."

"But I'm not." Sean rolled up his sleeve. "Is that why you got the tattoo? You wanted to blame all the murders on me?"

"Nice touch, wasn't it? Of course, it was just a temporary one I got in Santa Cruz that washed right off."

"You're dreaming, Jacoby. You can't pull this off."

He rested the barrel of his gun against Elise's temple. "You're going to jump off the Golden Gate Bridge, or I'll shoot Elise in the head and dump her over. Then I'll shoot you and dump your body over. Is that clear, Brody?"

"If you do it that way, it's going to spoil your little scenario."

"One way or the other, you'll both be dead. Who knows? You might survive the jump. I hear you need to go in feet first at an angle. You're even wearing heavy boots."

"Sean, don't even think about it."

Jacoby smacked Elise's other cheek and Sean almost went for him.

"Or I can slice and dice Elise while you watch, leave her body on the bridge and then shoot you. I'll figure it out, but it would be easier for you if you just jump. Now."

Sean took a step toward the guardrail. The wind lashed

his face. He'd make the SOB kill him here, unless he could get the gun away from him…and off of Elise.

"Sean, don't." Elise twisted away from Jacoby.

Jacoby raised his weapon, but Elise scrambled on top of the guardrail, throwing one leg over.

"Elise! What are you doing?"

Jacoby crowed and trained his gun on Elise straddling the guardrail. "I knew she'd die for you."

"If I jump, it's just you and him, Sean. And you're a superstar cop. He's just a guy who takes fingerprints."

And then she rolled over the edge.

Sean bellowed and rushed Jacoby, who'd lowered his weapon in momentary shock. Sean drove his shoulder into Jacoby's iron chest and twisted his arm back.

The gun dropped from Jacoby's hand and skittered across the cement. They both lunged for it, but Sean was taller with longer arms and reached it first. He tensed his body, waiting for Jacoby's attack, but felt nothing but cool air.

Gripping the gun, he rolled onto his back—just in time to see Jacoby go over the guardrail.

Sean staggered to his feet, sobs building in his chest, taking his breath away. Why had Elise done that? Why had she sacrificed herself for him?

"Sean!"

His stomach dropped. "Elise?"

"I'm down here, on the ledge."

Sean leaned over the guardrail. Elise was huddled on the two-foot-wide ledge. Warm relief poured through his body and he reached over the rail for her.

"My God, what did you do?"

"I knew the ledge was here. When I rolled over, I grabbed for these pipes to hold myself up and pulled myself to the ledge."

"Jacoby?"

"He went right over me. I hope he saw me before he started flying."

Sirens wailed in the distance.

"Now they get here." He extended his arms. "Hold on to me and I'll pull you over."

He clasped her arms and pulled her up until she was folded over the guardrail. She rolled onto the ground from there.

Sean sat down next to her because he didn't think he could stand another minute. He wrapped his arms around her and pulled her into his lap. "You plunged me into the deepest darkness I'd ever known before."

"I knew it would distract him enough for you to get the upper hand."

"A bit drastic, but then you go for the dramatic."

"I didn't see any other way." She snuggled against his chest as the sirens drew closer.

"You seem drawn to the bay, one way or another. Must be fate."

She placed her cold hands on each side of his face and pressed her lips against his. She whispered, "This is the only fate I want."

Epilogue

The music grew frenzied and someone smashed a plate.

Elise lightly scraped her fingernails across Sean's tattoo. "You told someone to do that."

He grabbed her hand and kissed her fingers. "You jumped off the Golden Gate Bridge for me. I can arrange for a few broken plates. But I've got a question for you."

"Fire away."

"Did you ever sign up for one of those online dating services?"

Her cheeks sported a pleasing pink. "No. Why would you think that?"

"The two other women who were murdered had profiles on Lovelines."

Elise wrinkled her nose as she spread more tapenade on a cracker. "Not unless…"

"Not unless what?"

"Courtney was teasing me about being dateless one night and threatened to register me." She put down her cracker and dropped her lashes. "Maybe she did it as a joke. It's something Courtney would do."

He brushed his fingertip across her cheek. "I'm sorry, but it looks like Courtney may have steered Jacoby into your life before you brought him into hers."

"It doesn't make it any better."

"I know. When you lose a friend, especially like that, the pain will come out of nowhere and strike you."

"And you know all about that."

"My pain has been fading a little more every day—because of you."

He cupped her face with one hand and nibbled on her earlobe.

Two of the waiters approached them and dragged them onto the dance floor, where they joined half the restaurant in a Greek dance that nobody knew.

Ten minutes later, laughing and breathless, they collapsed in their chairs. "Two months ago, you would've never seen me out there."

"If you hadn't brought attention to yourself by all that PDA, they never would've singled you out. You'd better learn the ropes. Sometimes, you're just asking for attention."

"And you know all about that, Runaway Bride. How's Ty doing back home?"

"He's fine. He has an amazing story to tell all the ladies and a missing finger to prove it, so he's lapping up all the attention."

Sean's cell phone buzzed in his pocket, and he pulled it out.

Elise touched his arm. "Everything okay?"

He held the display out to her. "It's my brother, Eric, the FBI agent. He was able to order some additional toxicology reports on Dr. Franklin, and he had a trace of some chemical in his bloodstream."

"Sean, that's great—I think. Is it great? It might prove someone murdered Dr. Franklin and it might have something to do with your father's case."

"Maybe it will, but my life isn't on hold anymore. I'll help Eric if he needs it, but right now I have some living to catch up on."

She grabbed his hands. "Great. Then let's get started, because there's something I've been wanting to do with you for a while now, and it's only eight o'clock, so we still have time."

"Really?" He gave her his best wicked grin.

"I want to take a walk with you on one of my favorite places in the city."

He tilted his head. "Let me guess—the bridge."

She nodded, her big blue eyes wide. "Are you in?"

"Let's go, but no jumping and no swimming in the bay."

"Got it."

Later, when they walked hand in hand across the bridge, the lights of the city twinkled in the mist and a boat skimmed beneath them.

Whatever drove his father, Sean knew he had a different destiny—and the brave, fearless woman beside him would be a part of it every step of the way.

* * * * *

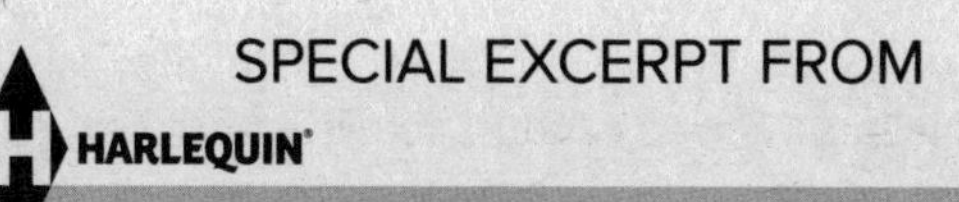

SAWYER

by USA TODAY *bestselling author*

Delores Fossen

A woman he'd spent one incredible night with and the baby who could be his will have Agent Sawyer Ryland fighting for a future he never imagined...

Agent Sawyer Ryland caught the movement from the corner of his eye, turned and saw the blonde pushing her way through the other guests who'd gathered for the wedding reception.

She wasn't hard to spot.

She was practically running, and she had a bundle of something gripped in front of her like a shield.

Sawyer's pulse kicked up a notch, and he automatically slid his hand inside his jacket and over his Glock. It was sad that his first response was to pull his firearm even at his own brother's wedding reception. Still, he'd been an FBI agent long enough—and had been shot too many times—that he lived by the code of better safe than sorry.

Or better safe than dead.

She stopped in the center of the barn that'd been decorated with hundreds of clear twinkling lights and flowers, and even though she was wearing dark sunglasses, Sawyer was pretty sure that her gaze rifled around. Obviously looking for someone. However, the looking around skidded to a halt when her attention landed on him.

"Sawyer," she said.

HIEXP69758

Because of the chattering guests and the fiddler sawing out some bluegrass, Sawyer didn't actually hear her speak his name. Instead, he saw it shape her trembling mouth. She yanked off the sunglasses, her gaze colliding with his.

"Cassidy O'Neal," he mumbled.

Yeah, it was her all right. Except she didn't much look like a pampered princess doll today in her jeans and body-swallowing gray T-shirt.

Despite the fact that he wasn't giving off any welcoming vibes whatsoever, Cassidy hurried to him. Her mouth was still trembling. Her dark green eyes rapidly blinking. There were beads of sweat on her forehead and upper lip despite the half dozen or so massive fans circulating air into the barn.

"I'm sorry," she said, and she thrust whatever she was carrying at him.

Sawyer didn't take it and backed up, but not before he caught a glimpse of the tiny hand gripping the white blanket.

A baby.

That put his heart right in his suddenly dry throat.

To find out what happens,
don't miss USA TODAY *bestselling author*
Delores Fossen's SAWYER, on sale in May 2014,
wherever Harlequin® Intrigue® books are sold!

HIEXP69758